BLIND ARROWS

Other Books by Anthony J. Quinn

The Blood–Dimmed Tide

The Inspector Celcius Daly Mysteries

Disappeared
Border Angels

BLIND
ARROWS

ANTHONY J. QUINN

NO EXIT PRESS

First published in 2015 by No Exit Press,
an imprint of Oldcastle Books Ltd,
PO Box 394, Harpenden,
Herts, AL5 1XJ, UK
noexit.co.uk
@noexitpress

Editor: Martin Fletcher

Written with the financial assistance of the Arts Council of Northern Ireland

© Anthony J. Quinn 2015

ISBN
978-1-84344-535-7 (Print)
978-1-84344-536-4 (Epub)
978-1-84344-537-1 (Kindle)
978-1-84344-538-8 (Pdf)

2 4 6 8 10 9 7 5 3 1

Typeset by Avocet Typeset, Somerton, Somerset TA11 6RT
in 12.5pt Ehrhardt
Printed in Great Britain by Clays Ltd, St Ives plc

For Lucy, Aine, Olivia and Brendan

ACKNOWLEDGEMENTS

I'd like to thank my agent Paul Feldstein for his tireless work, Martin Fletcher, my editor, for his invaluable contributions, and Ion Mills, Claire Watts and Frances Teehan at No Exit Press for doing a wonderful job in bringing this story to life. I'd also like to thank Damian Smyth and the Arts Council of Northern Ireland for their assistance. Finally, I extend my deepest gratitude to my wife Clare, and my children, Lucy, Aine, Olivia and Brendan.

ONE

Dublin, November 1919

Spies and lovers prosper by hiding in other people's secrets – the thought occurred to him while sitting in the sunroom of a half-empty hotel overlooking the beachfront at Bray. It was a wintry afternoon, and he had time and space to marshal his thoughts, stationed at the table next to the tall windows, sea spray obscuring the glass, a notebook at hand, and enough tea in a silver pot to keep the waiters at bay until the evening diners arrived.

Ever since starting his clandestine life, he had taken to visiting the beachfront several afternoons a week. He could feel safely alone here, removed from the war that was unravelling normal life in the heart of Dublin. Naturally, the sense of peace felt more pronounced inside the out-of-season hotel where the efficient bustle of the waiters seemed unconnected to things, to the city and its war, unconnected even to the sunroom and its forlorn backdrop of the sea.

He stirred his cup in the sunlight intensified by the broken, wavering sea, and thought again. *Perhaps we seek out the secret lives of strangers because we have grown tired of insulating our loved ones from the truth, or are spurred on by jealousy, since we understand that the less we know, the more decisively we can love.* He dangled his spoon in the cup and waited for the last thought to call up others, but the cold echo of the sea and the laughter of women and children gesticulating and playing along the promenade sent his thoughts scurrying into darker corners.

He looked up at the terraces of clouds moving across the sky, and waited, motionless, his troubled eyes giving themselves to the distant light. The clouds' sense of purpose and weightlessness made the room seem peaceful again. His mind continued with the train of thought. He composed the words and wrote them in his little leather notebook: *We are drawn to organise our secrets together, we spies in this war, our collections of broken vows and betrayals, the undetectable crimes of our guilty hearts...*

A large wave rose and came frowning over the promenade, chasing the figures from the beachfront. He poured himself another cup, and was reaching for the sugar, when the glass door swung open, and a woman in a wet fur coat entered, disturbing his cocoon of light and peace. The room filled with the rumble of the sea against the promenade. The linen cloths on the discreetly spaced tables rustled and lifted, and a blast of water droplets misted the air, leaving him conscious only of a fleeting translucence that was half sea–light, half skin as the woman's face floated towards him, his heart almost skipping a beat when she stopped at the table next to his. She slipped off her coat, revealing a figure of medium size in a long white dress. He glimpsed her profile: black hair framing a face so clean and delicate it looked as though it might have been found among the empty shells on the beach that morning. Nothing about her, however, struck him as forcibly as her dark eyes, secretly alert, observing him but appearing not to notice him as she composed herself at the table.

After ordering tea, she took out a book, and began to read. At first, he thought she might be waiting for a companion, but as the afternoon progressed, it became clear she was not expecting anyone. She seemed content to keep sitting with her book, barely changing the page, not raising her head once or glancing in his direction. There was something alluring and mysterious about the way she sat so close to him in the quiet room, the style of her black hair, the pale skin at the nape of her neck. She appeared not to notice his increasing stillness, his desire to discover more about her. When the gaslights came on along the promenade she rose and left without acknowledging his presence in any way.

He always took an interest in solitary female visitors to the hotel, and that evening he made enquiries about her. However, none of the staff knew her name. She did not belong to any of the well-to-do families in Dublin. One of the waiters thought she might work in Dublin Castle, the headquarters for the occupying British forces in Ireland, but beyond that, she was a complete stranger to everyone who worked there.

For the next couple of afternoons she returned to the sun-room, sat at the table next to him, and took out her book, quiet and reserved, avoiding eye-contact in her elegant, white dress, and giving no one cause to notice her, except him. She had captivated his attention completely now, with her long silences and her determined isolation. He knew that she would mean more to him than the other lonely women he had met: not just another isolated craving that ended abruptly in an anonymous bedroom. She sat so close to his table, he could feel the rhythm of her breathing, the curious calm that made her seem remote from everything else; her enticing presence in the pale afternoon as eerie as a flower that blooms only in mid-winter.

He tried to construct a personality, a life around her, a husband perhaps and children, but her solitary figure was immune to the powers of his imagination. He assumed that knowing the hotel's reputation, she had come to begin an affair, but then he began to think she was unhappy. She must be unhappy, he decided. From her slow movements, her disregard for company, and the way she stared at her book pretending to be engrossed in that same page for hours on end, he guessed that she was suffering from some private sadness.

When she left on the fourth day, he got up and followed her, taking with him his new silver-tipped cane for company. He had pursued women like her before, but never like this, not in the cold daylight of winter in full view of the hotel staffs' inquisitive eyes. For some reason his adventures seemed simpler and more amusing when conducted after the fall of darkness. He trailed her along the sea front and through the public gardens. He drummed out a tune with his cane on the cobblestones, but she seemed oblivious to it. She floated through the growing shadows of twilight without any sign of fear or caution. Not once did she give in to the temptation to look behind. She was like a serene fugitive from a doomed city, untroubled by the darkness gathering around her. Just as he was about to approach her, she slipped into a restaurant illuminated by orbs of streaming gaslight, and disappeared into a crowd of army officers and their wives. The military guard posted at the door blocked his way and demanded his papers. He walked away into the night, cleaving the air with his cane in frustration.

They seemed to go together, revolutionary wars and sad,

mysterious women. He was aware of their growing presence by the day, walking the streets of Dublin in a semi-trance, taking up tables in restaurants with their detached and martyred airs, staring through the windows of railway carriages, the rain-streaked glass magnifying their sadness, their doomed attachment to fallen men. However, something about the woman in the long white dress struck him as odd and separated her grief from the undifferentiated mass of misery flooding the city.

On the fifth afternoon, he found himself getting angry when she did not turn up at the usual time. He had arrived early, which added to his irritation. He tapped his cane impatiently against the leg of the table and ignored the waiter's inquiring presence. Then the glass door opened, and in she stepped without acknowledging his presence in any way. His anger abated when he saw that her face had been touchingly done up with make-up and powder. She glanced around the almost empty room as if searching for hints as to what she should do next. Slowly, deliberately, she chose the table next to his, took out her book and focused her attention on a single page.

After a while, rain drifted in from the sea. They looked up together, engrossed by the view from the windows, the deep distances dissolving in water and light, the deserted promenade swept away, the roar of the invisible waves drawing closer. He glanced sideways and saw that her figure had taken on an unreal, watery gleam. She was no longer a stranger but a symbol, another mystery at the heart of things, sitting close to him, lethal and silent, like a gun waiting to be fired. At last, he had found what he had been looking for – a woman with a secret to communicate.

He felt invigorated by the realisation and jumped from

his seat. She immediately placed her book on the table, as if to hide what she had been reading, and stared up at him, her eyes filling with alarm. She rose to a half-standing position but sank back when she saw him swing his cane through the air with deliberate aim.

With a flick of the cane, he knocked the book from her table. Then he bowed courteously and apologised. The look of alarm on her face intensified when he picked up the book and began inspecting the contents. It was a volume of Victorian poetry. A photograph slid from the page she had been reading. His curiosity increased. He stared at a picture of a child, a boy of about eight or nine, the corners worn away where it had been repeatedly touched, an invitation to sadness deeper than any poem.

He pulled up a seat and made some casual remarks about the afternoon light, the crashing waves, a few deft, indirect observations, giving her time to adjust to his intrusion, settle her emotions. He had no wish to intimidate or upset her. When the waiter appeared, he ordered some tea.

'Do you know who I am?' he asked, pouring her a cup.

She gave a little nod. Her face was sharply etched in the light of the tall windows.

'You're wondering what I want of you?'

'I'm almost afraid to ask.'

He sipped from his cup, and put it down next to hers. 'The reason I am here is to draw upon unusual means of support for my war.'

'Are the hush–hush men following me?'

'I wouldn't know.'

'You know where I work?'

'Yes.'

She risked a further question. 'Then am I in danger?'

'You misunderstand me. I am here to make you a proposal.'

'What sort of proposal?'

He tapped his cane on the photograph. 'Tell me about the boy. He bears a striking resemblance to you. Especially around the eyes. Perhaps he's a younger brother?'

She hesitated and stared at the picture, clenching her right hand in her lap.

He spread his hands. 'Pardon me; you don't have to tell me anything about the boy, if he is your dear brother or not.'

He was an effective interrogator. She rushed to correct him, explaining her relationship to the boy, without pausing to consider his professional technique, the deliberate mistake accompanied by a humble apology.

'Not my brother; my son.'

He nodded sympathetically, and she continued talking. She told him that her name was Lily Merrin, the daughter of a retired British Major. She had married at eighteen, but her husband had died in the Great War, leaving her to bring up their young son alone. She recounted the catastrophe that had further darkened her young widowhood, robbing her of her beloved son, how she had given up all hope of ever seeing him again.

If she was taken aback by the intensity of the questioning that followed, she did not show it. He made it clear he wanted to hear everything, guiding her through the background details of her life, her upbringing and education, her career and social circle. He did not show any surprise at her story. He knew about dark places, and the men who lived at the edges of the social order, the kidnappers and blackmailers, the spies and the informers, the saboteurs and the double-crossers.

The light faded from the sea, numbing the mood in the unlit sunroom. Rain began to fall, pecking the glass.

'Having your son taken away like this is the worst disaster that can befall a mother – like the end of the world.'

'I don't know how I'm meant to deal with it. At least death would have left fewer questions unanswered, less hope and fear in my heart.'

They sat for a while, sipping tea, watching the darkened clouds float in over a wintry sea. Their vista held little evidence of the dangerous revolution that had overtaken their city, no sense of a country pitching towards its doom, no connection to the ambushes, the bedroom raids, the bombing and shootings, the layered centuries of repression, the paralysis of a nation.

'The people who have taken away your son are efficient and ruthless,' he said in a controlled voice, not wishing to provoke her grief. 'They are fighting for the heart of this country. It is in their nature to destroy our children, our very name. You understand how dangerous it will be to have him returned to you?'

She nodded. He paused for thought, arranging her story in his head. He glanced at her face and was pleased to see that he had been shrewd in his choice. There were women he wanted to study from a distance, and there were others he absolutely had to pursue, the ones whose sadness gestured at him in interesting ways, who had a special daring, whose eyes shone with fierce secrets.

After careful consideration, he explained that he felt compelled to help her, but he needed to take certain precautions. Secrets became dangerous when shared with others. He smiled kindly.

'But, in the circumstances, your desire to be reunited

with your son fits in very well with my plans.'

At last, she made eye contact with him, steady and sustained, a blend of respect and fear.

She swallowed slightly. 'What is it you want me to do?'

He spoke gently. He wanted the two of them to develop a special relationship of trust, one that would take certain, interesting paths. He outlined some of the risks she would have to take. 'But trust me; everything will go according to my plan. When this war is over, in a few months' time, I will reunite you with your son, and then you will have your revenge. But first, you must wait and be patient.'

Her face sharpened at the mention of revenge. He recognised that look. He knew that there were betrayals in the wars between nations and entire continents that were infantile when compared to the betrayals of the human heart.

TWO

Lily Merrin, a typist employed by the British intelligence service, stood on the stone-flagged floor of First Section's archive in the cellars of Dublin Castle. The building was the nerve centre of Britain's colonial and military bureaucracy in Ireland, a fortified mass of granite stonework comprising a central block, a barracks and a rat-infested prison famous for its executions. She peered through the keyhole into the corridor, waited, paced up and down, waited, and then, as soon as the guard walked off, she flung open the door and ran down a darkly coiled staircase into a side courtyard visible only through the barred windows of the prisoners' cells. She would have preferred rain or blinding snow, anything that might have concealed her passage out of the castle and through the streets, but that afternoon the weather was dauntingly bright for December. Exiting through a door in the Liffey side of the outer wall, she could see, in the distance, a cordon of policemen blocking the monumental gateway to the castle, and the dark figure of a man in a long coat and riding boots leering at the queue of office girls being searched at gunpoint.

For a moment, she was at a loss what to do. She contemplated creeping back and returning the files, which she had secretly removed from the dusty stacks of the intelligence archive and hidden beneath her coat. The long shadows cast by the winter sun made the fortress seem more sepulchral than it was in reality, the windows and entrances eerily deep and dark. Its gloom seemed to reach out towards her like a pair of possessive hands eager to take back its secret knowledge.

She knew there was no way back now, and that she should hurry with her familiar lunchtime routine. The less energy and time she expended worrying about the dangers of what she had undertaken, the better for all concerned. The consequences of not carrying out the mission were so dire for her son, she could not jeopardise his safety by losing her nerve now. In any case, the guard might have returned to the archive section, removing any chance of safely replacing the files.

The heavy-set policemen worked their way through the queue of staff and visitors. She heard the rumble of their broad Ulster accents as they shouted out orders. They were predictable and concentrated in their efforts, like hunting dogs sniffing at every hole in the ground. She could tell that it was not a routine search from the nervous expressions of the workers and the behaviour of the man in the riding boots, whose presence, as he circled the policemen, had the effect of galvanising their efforts. They proceeded with increased urgency, working their way through the line, pulling roughly at coats, emptying handbags and briefcases, ushering a few of the secretaries back into the confines of the castle. The low sun fixed the scene like a moment from a nightmare.

Hearing footsteps approaching from behind, she stepped off in the opposite direction, tightening her handbag around her shoulder. To allay her anxiety she tried to imagine herself as a fragment of a larger picture, a shadow scuttling away from the main action, a page ripped from a book that no one dared to read. She did not know the importance of the files she had hidden beneath her coat, nor would she ever understand the repercussions of her actions. She had cast her eye over them briefly, seen the numbers and names, and wondered why they were so important. Her knowledge would always be incomplete; that was how Michael Collins, the IRA leader, and his intelligence men worked. It was for her protection as much as for theirs.

'Lily!' The male voice behind her spoke with devastating clarity and authority.

It was too late to look around. Pretending she had not heard, and without losing a fraction of her poise, she quickened her step, moving in the direction of the city centre. She heard the call repeated, and this time recognised the smooth military voice of her boss, General Jack Stapleton. Without a sideways glance, she veered towards the shadows cast by the high boundary walls, and ghosted along the bullet-pocked stonework towards Grafton Street. Very soon, the stream of pedestrians engulfed her on their way towards Dublin's teahouses and restaurants.

She hurried through the crowds, weaving an unplanned route through side streets; glancing back now and again to check that Stapleton's big military figure was not bounding after her. At the corner of Trinity Street, she stopped and tried to bring her breathing under control. She could not get used to the idea that what she was doing was the most serious form of treachery imaginable. She leaned against a lamppost, her head feeling dizzy.

Normally, she could have made her way to the anonymous boarding house on Victoria Way with her eyes shut tight, so carefully rehearsed was the fifteen-minute journey.

However, that afternoon her anxiety filled the city's streets and squares, making her unsure of her bearings, distorting her familiar route into a black maze. She felt oppressed by the sense that someone was watching and following her. She imagined herself stalked, not so much by the policemen, or Dublin Castle's spies, but by the looming fortress itself. The castle seemed fastened at the edge of her vision, towering above the jumble of Georgian terraces and thoroughfares. A church bell struck half past the hour. She ducked down a little side street, only to find the building sitting in the near distance, its dark mass floating in the bright sun, an ugly exhibition of shadows and secrecy. She turned her back on it, forcing herself not to think of its sinister influence, the turmoil of history that spilled through its gates, its daily disgorging of spies and assassins into a city that was filled this afternoon with the amiable chatter of salesgirls and the cries of market traders.

She found her bearings and rushed past the shops on Grafton Street without casting a glance at the windows full of shoes and winter clothes.

The sound of quick footsteps made her start and look round. She was relieved to see an irate shopkeeper in pursuit of a boy running with a brown bag. However, in his haste, the child ran straight into her, the force of the impact knocking her to her knees. A bunch of red apples emptied from the bag and rolled along the cobbled pavement. The boy stood stock-still, gazing at her anxious face. She drew in her breath. He was the very image of her son, only more wretched looking, with starved cheeks and eager eyes that chewed a hole in her heart. She reached out to stroke his face.

'Isaac?' she asked, uncertain of herself. It was the first

time she had mentioned her son's name in a month, but it wasn't him, not her dearest boy, whose image she kept alive in the most secret recesses of her heart. The boy saw her vulnerability, the unsteadiness in her legs, her eyes clouded by grief. Something strange and vicious ate at his face. He snatched at her handbag and tried to wrest it free. Emotion rose in her throat, thick and choking. Reaching out, she smacked his cheek so hard tears welled in his eyes.

The shopkeeper's burly arms intervened.

'For the love of God I'll strangle you,' he roared, grabbing the boy by the scruff of the neck. She blundered away from the commotion, moaning to herself, bumping heavily against people. The possibility that Collins had arranged for the child to collide with her on purpose flashed through her mind. He was always presenting her with tangible reminders of the inescapable power the Irish Republican Army held over her.

Someone blocked her path; a masculine, soldierly face with unblinking eyes. 'Are you all right?' he asked, in a clipped English accent like the general's. A crowd of curious pedestrians gathered close, threatening to entangle her further.

She felt for the files beneath her coat, and then pushed through the onlookers. Time was running out for her and her child.

'Excuse me,' said an angry voice.

'Watch where you're going,' shouted another.

'These people think they own the street,' they said, following her with their angry eyes.

She veered onto the road, and pulled back as an army truck, nosing its way through the horse-drawn carts, hooted at her. Sirens and similar truck signals echoed in the distance. She slipped back into the obscurity of a side street before emerging onto Lombard Street. From there it was only a short distance to her secret destination.

Her footsteps grew heavier as she approached the boarding house at 6 Victoria Way. The afternoon took on a greater coldness and depth, the brightness of the sky dissolving in the shadows cast by the three-storey building.

Assuming an air of ownership, she opened the unlocked front door and stepped inside. The hallway seemed as neglected as the exterior. She listened for signs of life and then climbed the stairs to a room on the first floor, a bleak room, empty of furniture apart from a small desk with a black typewriter and a seat in a corner. A clock and an untidy-looking notice board hung in front of the typewriter.

She was only in the room a minute, when she heard someone turn the key in the door, and the lock click into place. It was the first sign that afternoon of her normal routine, the sense that everything was proceeding smoothly. The IRA had chosen the room with care. They wanted her to be alone, undisturbed. She had been coming to the boarding house every lunchtime for the past fortnight and in all that time, she had not met anyone in the hallway or landing. Whoever held the key to the room was at great pains to protect her privacy.

She was half-relieved, half-saddened to see no letter waiting for her. She looked up at the board, which was covered in newspaper clippings, describing the mysterious disappearance of eight-year-old Isaac Merrin from his grandmother's home in England, the police investigation and the growing fears that he had been abducted. She pulled her coat tightly around her shoulders. The boarding house was cold. She had a sense of her life suspended, stopped in its tracks. The clock on the wall counted down the unfilled minutes of her lunch break. Eventually she pulled out the file of papers she had hidden in her coat, drew up the chair to the typewriter and began attacking the keys. Occasionally she stopped at the sound of a creak. Once, she rose and listened at the locked door. The house was submerged deep in silence.

She leaned over the typewriter, losing herself in the flurry of keys. There was no ambiguity about what she was doing. Her fingers did not hold back, punching out the details of the secret file, the financial transactions, the money moving from account to account, cash for guns, cash for ammunition, the names of beneficiaries, men-on-the-run, widowed families and prisoners' wives; an intelligence dossier on the republican army's finances, the numbers blurring past her.

When she had finished typing the document, she sealed it in an envelope and placed it in a drawer. She returned the original file to her inside coat pocket, stood up and put on her hat and coat. A button popped from her lapel and rolled into a crack in the floorboards. She spent several minutes searching for it, even though she risked being late. She never left behind a single trace that might link her to the room.

As was the usual routine, someone had unlocked the door. She stepped into the empty landing, hurried down the stairs, and walked out into the street. Her eyes watered in the winter light. She was aware of a few dim figures swimming on the periphery of her vision. She slowed her gait, trying to look at ease, but something felt wrong.

Everything depended upon her remaining calm, she told herself. She comforted herself with the assurance that she had one powerful ally left, the man with the silver-tipped cane. However, it was difficult to keep going with confidence when she felt so alone. She glanced behind her and saw a tall, dark figure bobbing towards her, followed by more shadows.

It seemed so theatrical to her, the brightness and the black approaching figures, the hushed street, the sound of her footsteps. As though the scene had been cleared of everything extraneous to the drama that was about to unfold. She glanced behind again, and made an anxious calculation as to how quickly the men were gaining on her. She wondered should she stop and surrender herself, but she was frightened of the world her pursuers represented, the corridors of prisoner cells and rooms full of intelligence files, a bottomless well of paranoia and suspicion, which she hated just as much as the empty boarding house room, its black typewriter and the key quietly turning in the door.

Ahead of her, she saw the figure of a man in a long coat climb into a hansom cab. He looked round at the last moment, and touched the brim of his hat, lowering it a little so that his eyes were shadowed. He seemed to acknowledge her presence. As he closed the door behind him, he swung a cane in the air, a silver-tipped cane glinting in the sunlight.

Finally, he had come, she thought with relief. She increased her pace, and immediately the footsteps behind her quickened. She heard an English voice call out her name. Trying not to alarm whoever they were, she kept a brisk pace, pretending not to hear. With difficulty, she resisted the impulse to break into a run. The cab moved off slowly, the driver pulling back the horses, giving her just enough time to jump in. Then he shook the reins and the team took off in a canter.

The curtains of the cab were drawn, and in the darkness

she leaned with a sigh of relief towards the outline of the man waiting for her.

'Thank God, you came. They must have followed me to the boarding house. I think our game is finally up.'

The shadowy figure gave a slight nod of the head. His movements were stiff and reserved. She could hear the hoarseness of his breath. She leaned closer, and brushed her fingers across his face, bringing her lips to his mouth, but something about his lack of responsiveness to her touch made her stop. It was neither shyness nor reserve, but something else. She felt an absence of feeling and warmth from his dark corner of the cab. She pulled back the curtains and took a sharp intake of breath. She saw a cold-faced stranger watching her intently. It wasn't the man she'd been expecting. This one was thinner and grey-eyed, treacherously gripping his silver-tipped cane. His face registered and analysed her shocked recoil.

'Driver, stop!' she shouted.

On the street behind them, a military-sounding voice roared a set of orders, and then a gunshot rang in the air, sending the horses into an out-of-control gallop. The shouting grew louder and then faded away. She turned to the door handle, pulling at it desperately, but it was locked. She lowered the window and thought of clambering out. The cobbled street rushed by at dizzying speed. She looked back at her fellow passenger; saw the outline of his body, its slowness, the vigour in his hands as he reached towards her, the features of his face changing, as hers had done, shifting through different emotions, different roles. A breeze blew against her face. She felt like she was falling endlessly through empty space.

THREE

It was just before eight o'clock on the evening of the Feast of the Annunciation, and Martin Kant, a *Daily Mirror* reporter, had battled the entire way from Dublin Castle through falling snow and throngs of mass-goers hurrying beneath the drifting flakes, their faces hungry but spirited looking after a day of prayer and religious fasting. A mood of fearful fanaticism had gripped the people of Dublin since the start of the war, and that evening church bells were pealing from every street corner – even the deepest stones in the castle's prison cells reverberated to their call.

It had not been cold enough for a frost and the big flakes of snow melted on the coats and faces of the faithful, and beneath their boots on the dark cobblestones of Merrion Square. From the belfry of St Teresa's Church came the soft chiming bells that signalled the prelude to eight o'clock mass. The snow fell thicker, coming in flurries, soaking and dissolving into the press of jostling bodies. In Kant's tired imagination, the crowd threatening to engulf him resembled a dark begging mouth feeding on the ghostly wafers of snow.

The mood reminded Kant of the first months of the Great War, when he had been a reporter behind enemy lines in northern France. Back then, he had established his reputation as a journalistic outlaw, a civilian in a grey coat secretly moving in and out of ransacked towns, amid the swarms of displaced people spilling from the train stations, collecting every type of rumour and news for the London press. The French churches had felt like safe havens, the one element of the evacuees' lives that remained permanent. The crowds in Merrion Square reminded him of the silent men and women gathering at church doors, mobilised by the rapture of their fear.

He realised he was late and pushed through the crowd with his silver-tipped walking cane. Amidst their incessant movement and the whirling flakes, he sensed something sinister, an impression of a black figure hastening behind him, agitated by something other than religious fervour. After the crowds had filed through the doors of St Teresa's Church and the streets emptied, the figure remained on the periphery of his vision, seemingly reluctant to draw closer. At the corner of Grafton Street, Kant dipped into the entrance of an alleyway and waited. The shadow hung back. He watched the snowflakes slowly melting into silence, a black bottomless silence that seemed to well up from the heart of the city.

The sight of a young woman in a fur hat and wrap hurrying towards his hiding place made him take a deep breath. In the glow of a streetlight, she faltered for a moment, unsure of where she was going. She ran past the entrance to the alleyway, the fleeting pressure of her feet barely disturbing the melting layer of snowflakes.

For a moment, he thought the woman might have been Lily Merrin, but a glimpse of her scarlet hair told him otherwise. It had been almost a week since she had accidentally kissed him in the darkness of the hansom cab, and he could still recall the press of her body, its forceful certainty, the sense of intrigue beyond his understanding.

He could feel the tingling sensation of her lips as she sought his mouth in the darkness, the taste of a hunted creature drunk on fear, and then her head pulling back, stung by the realisation that he was someone else. He remembered how the winter light had come flooding through the cab's curtains, revealing her anxious face, her mouth drawing in air, and then her grabbing at the door handle.

He hadn't talked about his encounter to anyone, not even his colleagues at Dublin Castle. At least, not yet. The entire events of that afternoon were like a dream he had had, and who ever confessed to kissing a strange woman in a dream? He thought of the meeting ahead and hoped he possessed the willpower not to speak to anyone about the incident. All he had to do was fill that gap in time with the details of another plot, another pursuit.

Once he was sure that the red-haired woman was not following him, he doubled-back and slipped into the Gresham Hotel on O'Connell Street. The lounge bar was almost full, but upstairs, in the guest bar, the only occupants were huddled at a table in front of a large bay window. A few of the men raised their eyebrows and muttered greetings as he pulled up a seat. He was the only reporter invited to these clandestine meetings, and he instinctively felt the group draw closer together as if to shepherd away the secrets they had been discussing.

The man dressed in a civilian suit at the top of the table gave Kant the most lacklustre welcome. General Jack Stapleton seemed at best indifferent to the reporter's arrival, if not perturbed by it. The head of British Intelligence at Dublin Castle, he needed neither uniform nor medals to announce the fact that he was a military leader. His face was lined with colonial wrinkles, his greying hair combed back from his forehead in two smooth bands, his chest upright, his moustache clipped, and his grey eyes sharp and straight. He stared hard at the reporter as if he was a stranger, his automatic recoil barely disguised. Eventually, some form of recognition must have dawned upon him, for he gave the reporter a barely perceptible nod, and went back to addressing the table.

Seated opposite the general was Corporal Derek Isham, head of Special Branch at Dublin Castle. The corporal smiled at Kant. It wasn't a charming smile. Kant saw arrogance and scorn curl the corners of his mouth, and in his eyes, something else, something thwarted and dark.

The other faces at the table belonged to the hush-hush men, common spies, watchful suspicious faces. Ex-convicts, former soldiers, adventurers and mercenaries, some of whom were missing fingers or carried scars. They eyed each other in the way a grotesque man glances at himself in a mirror, searching for a less gruesome reflection, a more accommodating angle.

These irregular meetings in the Gresham Hotel were known as the Crow Club, although none of the men were bird-lovers. The name sprang from a joke at the general's expense – his orders made plenty of noise, but quite often little sense, and the shadowy group of spies he had assembled to prowl the streets of Dublin had cheerfully adopted it. The general had originally thought it a shrewd move to recruit a reporter like Kant to the club, encouraging him to bring details of the stories his colleagues were working on, and in return the general fed the *Daily Mirror* reporter pieces of propaganda to disseminate through the newspaper offices of the big London titles.

It went entirely against the point of good journalism, but

then the Irish War of Independence was a tangled conflict, and Kant, jaded from salvaging truth and colour from the battle fronts in western and eastern Europe, had craved a taste of adventure himself, a desire sharpened by the fact that his doctor had recently decided he was suffering from consumption. The diagnosis did not worry him unduly; his older brother had lived with the disease for more than ten years. What concerned him was the dread that he was suffering from something else, an inner restlessness more destabilising than tuberculosis. Before taking the Dublin post, he had briefly thought of fleeing to a monastery or becoming a missionary. He had even considered joining a revolutionary movement such as the Bolsheviks. The truth was that sometime during 1919, he had grown tired of the ordinary reporter's life he had returned to in London. He wanted to remain a journalistic outlaw, an in-between, not quite committed to the daily routine of work and family life. He wanted to come and go as he pleased in a mood of subterfuge, adopt a new name, a fictitious past, a cover story to avoid being discovered by hidden enemies, and what better place to do it than in the Dublin of 1919, a city that had become the settling pond for the dregs of the Great War.

There was nothing new in the Crow Club's discussion that night. The same rumours and suspicions about the IRA and the whereabouts of its leader Michael Collins that had been floating in the air since winter began. Evidence of the search for Collins, whom the British had branded the most wanted man in Europe, was everywhere in Dublin, the reward posters flapping at every train station, the news of his latest exploits shouted by newspaper vendors and filling column after column of leaded type, sweeping to the back pages news of war and famine, Russian revolutions and presidential elections. Collins' details had been circulated among the country's entire population of policemen and soldiers. It should have been impossible to escape the scouring attention of so many loyal and armed men.

'I've been studying your reports,' the general gruffly told the Crow Club. 'As a result of your tip-offs in the last month, my men have raided 27 boarding houses, and arrested 18 individuals suspected of belonging to the IRA. I've counted them all up. Not one of them has brought us any closer to catching Collins.'

'We've turned Dublin's hotels and boarding houses into busy hives of spies and informers,' explained Isham, 'but as soon as we find any trace of Collins, he vanishes.'

'Then does it upset you, corporal, that a Cork gombeen has made your mission a regular farce?' asked the general.

Isham caught Stapleton's grey eyes. 'What do you think?' His voice grew taut. 'Collins has made his life an enigma and fools of us all.'

For the Crow Club, finding the IRA leader was proving more difficult than trapping the invisible particles of air. He appeared to be made from an element that was undetectable to the eyes of Isham and his fellow Englishmen. He was the mystery they could not fathom; the plot they could not penetrate. He might even be among the clientele in the bar below; however, they did not know the secret signs that would reveal his whereabouts.

'What else can we do?' asked Isham. 'My men have pulled in all the suspicious looking fellows from the street. We've combed the boarding houses, cleared out the slum tenements, raided the bars and watering holes.' The dark rings beneath his eyes were evident in the dim light. 'We have been carrying out our duties to the best of our abilities in spite of the severe constraints.'

For the next half an hour, they discussed the hunt for Collins. Kant could not find a way into the conversation. He was lost for something to say. Instead, he found himself transfixed by the sight of the snowflakes falling against the window, their lengthening streaks against the darkness. He felt a cold draught penetrate the air, and it seemed to him that the flakes were seeping through the glass, drifting towards him. A familiar pain rose in his chest. Suppressing a coughing fit, he sank back into his seat, seeking comfort in the memory of the mysterious woman who had kissed him with such desperation in the hansom cab. Slowly, the coarseness and anger of the Crow Club began to dissolve, and a warm darkness folded itself around him, full of her breathless presence, her fingers and lips seeking him out, her body leaning across the heavy belt of his greatcoat, her touch warming the nape of his neck.

He sighed to himself. Her appearance in the cab had been so sudden, her intimacy so agile and disconcerting, she had rendered him defenceless. He was a war correspondent, and had survived months as an outlaw at the front lines, sending back uncensored reports while shells exploded around him and soldiers' smoking bodies disintegrated into the French mud. He should have been immune to her touch, not dazzled like a lovesick 16-year-old.

A prolonged silence among the members of the Crow Club wrenched him from his reverie. He had only been daydreaming a moment or two, and was unsure of when the atmosphere in the group had changed. Somehow, he had missed the glance or word that had stopped the discussion.

The general broke the silence with a hoarse voice: 'While you are still spies in the pay of the British Crown you must obey the rules of the intelligence game.'

'And what are those rules?' asked Isham.

'Whatever I damn well please.'

The men of the Crow Club looked at each other gloomily. Their eyes shifted in the glare of Stapleton's anger.

'Your job as agents of the Crown is to collect information and bring it to Dublin Castle. There your commanders will analyse it and make the correct political decisions.'

'A good agent should make his own decisions,' snapped Isham. 'He should carry out his own plans. We operate at the centre of extremely dangerous events.'

'None of you is entitled to influence the future of this country to that degree. Your actions are subordinate to a political course that has been chartered in advance.'

'Then the danger is Dublin Castle will be overwhelmed with an abundance of information,' said Isham. 'An intelligence agent should be allowed to find the most expedient solution when a problem or opportunity presents itself.' He lifted his empty glass and waved it at a waitress.

The general looked at him with a wary expression.

'What do you mean?'

By now, the spies had turned their attention to Isham, their cautious, ingratiating faces like cats around a saucer. Thornton, a Cockney ex-soldier, leaned forward.

'We should be given permission to kill Collins,' he hissed.

The general squinted at him. 'I've already made it clear that Collins should be arrested, preferably without injury to his person. Certainly not killed.'

'Let us embark in combat with Collins, sir,' pleaded Thornton. 'We are at the end of our tethers, collecting snippets of information and feeding them back to Dublin Castle. By the time your department organises a raid or search party Collins and his men have long flown the nest.'

'I echo his complaint,' said Isham. 'My men are itching to shoot the IRA leader on sight. And every one of his murderous accomplices. Give us the go-ahead, otherwise, prepare for us to stay here forever, and send us a bottle of whiskey each for the duration.'

Isham grinned and the table of spies added their guffaws. It was hard to tell whether it was the suggestion of free alcohol or Collins' murder that had induced their good humour.

Thornton's throat grew thick with spittle. 'I'd like to slip into Collins' bedroom at night with a knife between my teeth and stick him like a pig.'

'I'd kill him with a bomb,' said a hollow-faced Scot called Riley. 'Like Alexander the Russian king.' A rush of exhilaration animated his pale face.

'That's a clumsy and savage means of assassination,' said Isham. 'But even the world's greatest escapologist would have trouble crawling out of a crater filled with rubble.' He turned to the bar. Shaking his empty glass, he shouted, 'Can a gentleman not get a drink?'

'What kind of man slays his enemy with a bomb?' The general's eyes flashed at the table of spies. 'Can you imagine the political scandal if the explosion harmed women or children? God in heaven, what would the foreign press make of it?' He glanced uneasily at Kant. More calmly, he added, 'No, we must eliminate the threat posed by Collins in a more efficient manner.'

'Poison,' suggested Riley cheerfully. 'Or shall we just smash in his brain box?'

Another voice spoke from the middle of the table. 'I propose we take him from his bed, and carry him blindfolded to Dublin Castle where we'll hang him from the gallows ourselves.'

Outside the snow kept on falling, colliding with the darkness, hordes of flakes thickening against the glass. The idea of Collins' murder was now firmly entrenched in the spies' imaginations.

'Listen to me carefully,' ordered the general. 'Collins is only 26 years old and yet he's achieved things that many generals never manage in an entire military career.' His voice quietened, and he gave a slight smile. 'Success changes a soldier; it makes him vulnerable.'

'How?'

'Men with gilded reputations like Collins' come down in flames very quickly. Do you know why?'

The spies listened intently.

'Because people like to see them fail,' said the general. 'Not only their enemies but also their comrades, the ones they call their closest friends. I imagine there are plenty of people on the sidelines of the IRA who would like to see Collins a broken man.'

'What do you propose we do?'

'I want you to subject Collins' closest associates to the most thorough observation. It is a fact of human nature that at least one of them will be prepared to betray or undermine him in order to advance his own position. It is the same as any political game.'

'We are men of action,' said Isham. 'Not political intriguers or gossip-mongers.'

'I insist we shall have no unnecessary killing. Men of your generation have seen too many deaths. Instead, my dear fellows, I want you to settle into Dublin life, frequent the bars and hotels. Strike up acquaintance with Republicans instead of killing them. Communicate with their secret cells. Pry into their private lives. I want to know what cigarettes they smoke, their favourite tipples, their habits and dress size, what debts they owe, their domestic situations, any history of alcoholism or insanity in their families.'

The spies hung over the table, their eyes expressing doubt at the general's directive.

'It sounds to me that it's a sketch artist you want,' replied Isham.

The men laughed again and turned their attention to the waitress, who was busy replenishing their glasses.

Kant watched Stapleton staring grimly at the uninhibited committee of spies and informers. The general appeared at a loss to control them. He ran his fingers over the white linen of the tablecloth as though searching for an escape in familiar luxuries. He caught Kant's stare and scrutinised him for several moments.

It struck Kant that, if there was a network of English spies in Dublin, it existed not as a functioning organisation but as a law unto itself, and the general had little control over its actions and their timing. In spite of his sympathy for the general, he could understand the Crow Club's frustration and impatience. Michael Collins was a void and they were a horde of spies falling without a place to land. If they had been soldiers in the trenches, they could have fought their foe face to face. But where was the enemy they must eventually fight it out with? A faceless figure pushing a bicycle into the twilight mist; an office clerk hiding behind a labyrinth of files; a gunman slipping into the bewildering sea of faces filling Dublin's busy streets. There was no longer a battlefield, an arena to engage the enemy, just this sense of endlessly drifting downward into darkness, like blind arrows, like snowflakes descending from the night sky.

'What are you doing here, Kant?' The general's sharp voice interrupted his thoughts.

The reporter cleared his throat. 'You asked me, sir, to bring you any reports of missing or murdered women. You said there was something important you wanted to discuss.' He removed a folder from his jacket and passed it across the beer-stained table.

'Of course, I remember,' said the general. He gathered up the reports and began reading them.

At one point, the general's puzzled gaze hovered over Kant, and then he returned to the papers. He looked back through them as if searching for something he might have missed. He rubbed his forehead and said nothing. The furrows of his brow deepened.

After a long pause, Kant asked, 'Sir?'

Stapleton turned his tired eyes to the reporter. He took a long mouthful of gin.

'Something distracts me,' he explained.

The general's discomfort ignited Isham's interest. 'Perhaps Mr Kant would care to share his little list with the rest of us,' he said.

Kant began to describe the gist of his findings, including the dead body he had viewed that evening in the hospital morgue. He spared no details, and for the first time the entire table directed his attention at him. Isham watched him, smug and amused, while the other spies listened with an air of bestial expectation.

'The dead woman, 24-year-old Susan O'Brien, had been a prisoner at Dublin Castle but was reported to have escaped on Sunday evening. Less than 24 hours later, her body was found lying face up in a forest south of Dublin. The police know very little about what happened to her. Her clothes were torn and her body badly mutilated. The unusual thing was that her eyes had been attacked in a very brutal way and her eyeballs removed. The police have no clues as to who murdered her, or why. At the minute, they are simply trying to figure out how. They've found no evidence of footprints or wheel marks in the snow around the body. Just the victim's footprints and the paw marks of what might have been dogs or foxes. It is no exaggeration to say that the entire occurrence of her death is a complete mystery to them.'

Kant went on to describe how the body of another woman had been found in similar circumstances the week before. 'Police believe the unidentified victim had been led to the forest clearing by a lust murderer. But, yet again, the perpetrator left no evidence of his presence. Her eyeballs had also been gruesomely removed.'

'What colour was her hair?' asked the general.

'Red and long,' replied Kant.

'The full Celtic mane,' remarked Isham with a little smile.

Stapleton stared hard at his corporal.

'I've also included in the file a series of newspaper clippings describing a number of missing women,' Kant continued. 'Several of whom had been suspected of helping the IRA.' He ran through the names. 'Aileen Keogh, a nurse at Mount St Benedict School, arrested for possession of an incendiary device. Rosaleen O'Neill, an artist's model, captured driving a car load of IRA members. 16-year-old Mary Bowles who had been sentenced for trying to hide an IRA machine gun from Crown Forces. Madeline Mullan, arrested for keeping a military patrol under surveillance. All of the women vanished while being held in custody at Dublin Castle.'

'You mean they escaped and went on the run,' said Isham. 'They didn't just disappear like rabbits down a hole in their cells.'

'According to the prison guards and the police there were no clues as to how they escaped from custody,' said Kant. 'No evidence of a conspiracy to free them. Their families have mounted a prayer vigil at the prison gates, demanding news of their whereabouts.'

There was a long silence. Kant snatched a glance at the general, who had closed his eyes and was breathing heavily. He eyed him closely, and wondered had the general consumed too much drink? In fact, everyone at the table looked as though they had drunk too much. He took in the emptiness of their glaring eyes, the snow swirling in the darkness of the bay windows behind them.

The general roused himself with a growl and ordered more gin. 'I want you to investigate what happened to these women, Mr Kant. Use your journalistic contacts and dig deep. Find out how they disappeared from prison.'

Isham leaned towards the general with a sardonic grin. 'There's more to this. You haven't dragged Mr Kant here out of concern for a few fugitive IRA women.'

The general cleared his throat. 'Of course, there's more.' He raised his glass to his mouth and a little gin accidentally sloshed over the rim. 'There's another name I must add to the list.' He hesitated. 'A young woman called Lily Merrin. She was one of my secretaries at Dublin Castle. She went missing a week ago during her lunch break. And hasn't been spotted since.'

'Have you reported this to the police?' asked Isham.

Again, the general's brow appeared to tremble. 'The local constabulary is not equipped to carry out such a sensitive investigation. They're Irish and stupid and riddled with informers.' He sighed. 'Their main talents appear to be collecting gossip and burning down houses.' He turned to Kant. 'I want you to find out what is happening to these missing women, and in particular Merrin. Quietly. Without drawing too much attention.'

Kant's neck and cheeks were itching. 'Anything could have happened to these women, sir,' he suggested. 'They may have emigrated to America, or eloped with someone. Perhaps they had a domestic or family problem.'

'I still want to know.'

'Merrin had access to intelligence files in Dublin Castle,' said Thornton. 'Perhaps she's another IRA spy on the run.'

The general's face coloured with anger. 'I order you to keep a decent tongue in your mouth when speaking about this woman. Her loyalty is beyond doubt; she is from the very best Anglo-Irish stock. Her father was a general in the British Army, and her husband died at the Somme.'

Kant felt another urge to scratch his neck.

Isham grinned and winked at the others. 'Army men always worry more about their mistresses than their wives. If you only knew the number of times I've wondered what my Poppy is up to.'

The alcohol began to do its work, and the conversation strayed onto the subject of Irish girls. Kant stared at the circle of faces boasting of the women they had enjoyed. His head ached and the smell of gin and whiskey crawled up his nose. He was struck by the flushed ugliness of his drinking companions, the coarseness of their conversation, their spurious tales of lust and conquest. Their gloating eyes alienated him. God damn them for their boasting and lying, he thought. They made Dublin sound like the most whorish city in the world where the laws of supply and demand governed every encounter with its female inhabitants.

His chief problem was how to tell the general that he had shared a hansom cab with his missing secretary on the day she had disappeared, that he had seen her inconsolable with fear. He looked at his hands, one gripping his glass, the other the hat on his knee. His tale would go against him very badly, he realised, since he could offer no innocent explanation as to why he had been trailing her that afternoon.

The part of the day he preferred to recall was that moment of unexpected intimacy in the darkened cab. It had a dramatic quality that foreshadowed the rest of the afternoon, the two of them safe and enclosed in the silence with just a crack of winter light creeping under the curtained windows, his neck and scalp tingling where she had just touched him, and then the lingering precision of her lips on his cheek, her breath sweet and clean. He tried to seal the moment up in that hushed chamber, keep it intact forever. He felt a strange happiness flood through him. Their encounter had been something to treasure, a jewel in the casket of the cab, and he felt an urgent need to reveal it to the general, but his caution held him back. He knew he ought to have warned Merrin, revealed who he was and why he was following her, but he had been unable to say a word. He passed his hand over his face, still feeling the astonishment at being kissed by a frightened, dangerous woman. He might have bartered everything to be the man she thought he was, cast his subterfuge to one side, risked his safety, warned her that Dublin Castle reacted with ruthless justice to betrayal, especially when the traitor was one of their own.

Thornton elbowed him. 'What's bothering you, Kant? You look out of sorts.'

He smiled and tried to keep a prudent control of his tongue.

'I haven't seen you at the boarding house for days. The landlady thought you'd returned to London.'

Riley chipped in. 'He must have a woman hidden away in a hotel room somewhere. I recognise that look in his eyes.'

'You know very well that I couldn't afford to keep any woman in a hotel room,' replied Kant.

'Then it's a girl locked up in a back-street boarding house.'

'What we all need is a big house like Corporal Isham's,' whispered Thornton. 'One that has no prying landladies, only subservient Irish maids and lots of empty rooms.'

They looked at Isham's bored-looking face, colder and calmer than the general's but somehow less civilised. Kant had heard reports of how the corporal had requisitioned Park House, a seventeenth-century mansion with private grounds in the Wicklow Mountains. Every weekend, he organised hunts and parties for Dublin's ruling classes and its military commanders so that they could wallow in the luxury and glory of the Protestant Ascendancy, shooting pheasants and deer, while IRA guerrillas ambushed their foot soldiers in the city's back streets.

'Mr Kant is uncomfortable with all this talk of women,' said Riley. 'He must be married with a little wife in suburban London who knows nothing of his secret life in Dublin.'

The reporter shuddered at their line of questioning.

'My relationship with women changed during the Great

War,' he said. A spasm twitching his lips. Still that memory of Lily Merrin's kiss, a furtive little pleasure.

'What do you mean?'

'I can no longer ignore the fact that I am an ill man. And that instinctive love is beyond my reach.'

'Are you saying all you feel is lust?'

'I am not an animal.'

'Neither am I, but I would like to be an animal. Just for tonight. To revert to nature, to prowl through these bars and take what I want.'

Perhaps we are all animals, thought Kant, we survivors of the Great War, damaged creatures with the minds of monsters, without any hope of refuge from our base instincts.

'We are here because of work,' Thornton reminded them. 'Let's not mix it with pleasure.'

'I've had enough of work,' replied Riley, with vehemence. 'When do we enjoy the pleasure?'

Kant broke into a racking coughing fit. When he had finished, he looked across and saw the general's drunken eyes staring at him.

'You work for the *Daily Mirror*, is that correct?'

He cleared his throat. 'Their war correspondent, yes.'

'War.' Stapleton pronounced the word without irony or sadness. He lifted his chin, as though the last glass of gin had revived him. 'Did you enjoy reporting on the carnage at Ypres?' he asked.

'It was my job.'

'Your *Daily Mirror* sketches were very popular with readers. People tend to be drawn to accounts of suffering. Especially when perused from the safety of their own homes. Your reports fascinated and repelled them.' Stapleton took another sip of gin and his eyes moistened. He gave a sour laugh. 'We tried to censor reporters like you, but somehow the truth trickled out, like water from a poisoned well.'

From the bar below, a drunken woman gave a ludicrous high-pitched laugh.

When Stapleton began to speak again, he did so with the exaggerated speech of a drunken man disguising his slur.

'They tell me that you are one of the most tenacious reporters in England, Mr Kant. If there is a lust murderer on the loose, I want you to bring me a sketch of the beast.'

Kant nodded. It was past midnight and Dublin's dimensions were changing under the falling snow, swelling and leaning closer to the bay windows, like a familiar face in a suffocating dream.

Isham turned to him. 'Mr Kant is one of those reporters who hide themselves very well. I believe he might just be the very man we need.'

'What do you mean?' asked Kant.

'You're easily overlooked. Like a shadow that blends into the greyness.'

'It's something I've learned to use to my advantage.'

Isham waited until the general returned to his gin. He leaned closer with a more serious expression on his face.

'You must meet me tomorrow morning at 6 Victoria Way,' he whispered. 'I've some important information that will assist your search. I can reveal a secret the general doesn't know about his treacherous little secretary.'

Kant felt a strong desire to confess that he knew the significance of the house number, that he had seen Merrin hurry from it on the day she disappeared. It was unwise, but he had a passion to unburden himself to someone, to disclose that he knew Merrin, and that he had spent a very private moment with her, but at the last moment, something in Isham's eyes discouraged him.

Kant grabbed his hat and stood up. Rather than saluting, he nodded with professional courtesy at the two military men and took his leave from the Crow Club. Gripping his cane for assistance, he left the hotel and set off into streets paved in white, lengthening into the night. The impulse that drove him into the dark heart of the city wasn't patriotic duty: it was desire leading him on, the hope of recovering the warm memory of Merrin's touch and kiss, the hunger in her searching fingers and lips, the sensation of a strange and frightened woman seeking his protection, a refuge that was not his to give.

FOUR

Corporal Isham's face usually wore a sardonic expression, but the next morning his eyes were glistening with excitement. 'I enjoy chasing women myself, but only for sport, you understand,' he told Kant. 'However, I don't think I've ever pursued a woman quite as intriguing as the general's Lily Merrin.'

Dressed in a short coat and black riding boots, he opened the door at Number 6, Victoria Way. He drew Kant up the unlit stairs to a room that was empty apart from a desk, a typewriter, a chair and a notice board covered in faded newspaper clippings and letters.

'Do you ever watch women, Kant? I mean steadily watch them day and night. There are many things you can learn from watching women go about their secret business.'

Kant felt uneasy, but stood still, wary of Isham and the little room beckoning before him. He closed his eyes for a moment. There was no sound, no smell, nothing that might bring him back to the hushed hansom cab and his memory of Merrin's caress, just a sense of danger radiating from the direction of the desk and the black typewriter.

'A month ago, we began to suspect the IRA might have a mole in Dublin Castle,' explained Isham. 'So we began to follow the movements of all the staff who had access to intelligence information.'

Kant opened his eyes and watched the corporal glide across the floor, quick and fluid as a shadow.

'We discovered that Stapleton's secretary was spending her lunchtimes grabbing as many secret documents as she could from Dublin Castle's intelligence files. Then she'd dash up to this room where she typed out copies, sealed them in an envelope and left them for the IRA to collect.' Isham hovered over the desk.

'What sort of material did she give them?'

'Enough to break our network of spies and send good men to their deaths. From now on we're restricting security clearance and placing the most sensitive documents in crypto-code.'

Isham bent over the typewriter, blew on the dusty keys, and used his handkerchief to lift a long dark hair. 'We've interrogated the landlady. Her instructions were to lock the door once Merrin began typing. Then, ten minutes before two, unlock it. Her lunchtime caller was her only guest. All the rooms were kept empty of lodgers.'

He waved Kant over to the desk. The reporter almost crept towards it, feeling the presence of Merrin. The typewriter floated before him, a metal nest with its litter of keys, not just a machine to print correspondence but an instrument of treachery and death.

Isham laughed in a cold way. 'The general's little secretary was the IRA's most motivated spy. Devoted to betrayal. I imagine she would have filled this entire room with pages of freshly typed intelligence until they spilled down the stairs and out the front door. A house full of secrets. Enough to destroy Dublin Castle for good.' He struck a key of the typewriter and its prong snapped upon the empty roller.

'What makes you say that?' It wasn't that Kant hadn't

suspected the full truth about Merrin, but part of him was still propped in a corner of the hansom cab, cramped and fumbling, weak to her caress and kiss. He needed Isham to fill in the spaces in his understanding, clear away the discrepancies.

Isham stared straight at him. 'Very few people are suited to the life of a secret agent. Most recruits turn out to be little more than foolish amateurs, or cowards and scatterbrains who think spying is like playing a game of cards or reading a suspense novel. In reality, it is a form of death. An entire life led in the shadows. The most successful agents like Merrin are those who develop an inner sense of purpose, whose souls are nourished by their spymasters.'

'And what was Merrin's nourishment?'

Isham pointed to the notice board. 'Newspaper clippings describing the IRA's abduction of her son. Letters in the boy's handwriting describing how his captors were looking after him. The only sustenance a desperate mother required.'

For the first time, Kant took in the contents of the board. The press reports told the story of how an eight-year-old boy called Isaac Merrin had gone missing whilst visiting his grandparents in England. Kant read about the initial police investigation, the sighting of two men with strong Irish accents in the vicinity of the grandparents' home, the growing fear that he had been murdered, detectives assigned to the case, and possible sightings along the length and breadth of Britain. He scanned the blue-coloured pages of the letters, a few smudged sentences in childish longhand describing the boy's captivity in a damp cottage somewhere by the sea. The wretched spelling moved him. Merrin's betrayal took on a responsibility, a moral force, which quickened his breath and made the blood in his head pound.

A vulnerable child was involved, the victim of a kidnap plot. The IRA had used the most compelling motivation possible to turn Merrin into a spy. They had emotionally blackmailed her with her son's letters, this mess of words scrawled across blue writing paper.

'The board was positioned so that the typist was forced to look directly at the letters,' continued Isham. 'Those IRA bastards kept the story of her boy's kidnap inches away from her nose. For an hour every day, they sealed her up with her grief. It must have been worse than physical torture.'

Kant saw that Collins did not need guns or bombs. He did not need ammunition to win his war. His was a silent struggle fought by spies like Lily Merrin. Women who carried a quiet desperation and determination in their daily lives, women typing their secrets in anonymous boarding house rooms, locked into a process, an underground intelligence system. The question was how long could Merrin's soul have survived on such meagre nourishment? How long before her maternal drive was whittled away by the constant betrayal and subterfuge? She was just one woman, surrounded by people who might expose her secret life at any moment, her nerve constantly tested.

'What would the IRA have done if she refused to give away intelligence?' asked Kant.

'Knowing Collins and his men, her son's letters would immediately stop. Instead she'd get a cut-off toe or finger.'

The door tugged open slightly, letting in a draught, and then slid shut again. They both listened to the house creaking back into silence.

'Then we cannot judge her by normal standards of right or wrong,' said Kant. 'A mother's longing for her son can sweep aside everything else, loyalty, the proud history of a family, even one's duty to the King. Whatever she did, it was done out of desperation. She wasn't a traitor. Just a mother in the wrong place at the wrong time.'

'At least she's no longer a threat we have to worry about.' Isham seemed unconcerned about her current whereabouts or safety.

Kant stared at the typewriter. He thought of Merrin hunched over the machine, fingers striking the keys, the prongs rising and falling, spelling out a life and death terrain of secrets, her fingers driving deeper into the keyboard, the prongs hammering quicker and quicker. He saw that the typewriter had been her only source of protection, a place to hide from her grief and anxiety, but one letter out of place and she might slip into the void forever.

'The puzzle for you, Mr Kant, is working out what happened to her that afternoon.'

'Perhaps instead of returning to Dublin Castle she thought it better to disappear. Before she could betray any more of her people.'

Isham shook his head. 'I believe someone at Dublin Castle let slip we were watching her. I had my men positioned that day to arrest her when she left the boarding house, but at the last moment, an accomplice turned up in a hansom cab and whisked her to safety. The general doesn't know this, but I've launched an internal investigation to uncover the suspected infiltrator.'

Kant now understood the dramatic events that had brought Merrin and him together. He remembered the sharp English voice shouting 'halt', followed by the retort of the gun that had spooked the horses into a breakneck gallop. He wondered should he tell Isham what had happened afterwards inside the hansom cab. It was a secret, but not one he wished to become a burden. Unfortunately, he had kept it to himself for too long, and in the circumstances, he knew the delay would arouse the prejudiced suspicions of Dublin Castle.

He avoided Isham's hard eyes. He turned and perused the notice board one more time, the blueprint of Merrin's betrayal.

'The last letter from the boy was sent more than three weeks ago,' he remarked. 'Up to that point she'd been getting one every week.' It was the only evidence he could find of what might have prompted the crucial turn her career as a reluctant spy had taken.

'Do you think the boy is still alive?' he asked.

The corporal gave a barely perceptible shrug. 'Keeping hostages alive can be quite a bother for terrorists. Especially a child. They have to be moved all the time, fed and looked after, at least in the basic ways.'

He gave Kant a penetrating stare. 'You are moved by her predicament?'

'Of course I am.'

'As a reporter searching for a scoop, or as a human being?'

'As a human being.'

'Then I must warn you to be more professional,' he said, his face blank and cold. 'This woman might end up ruining the career of General Stapleton. Even now, the old fool still believes she could do no wrong. I've watched him playing around with pretty young secretaries before. The devotion he shows them has earned him nothing but contempt from his fellow staff. Merrin was one of those girls who knew how to handle men's weaknesses. The last thing we need is a *Daily Mirror* reporter also in her thrall.'

He walked out of the room and Kant followed. The

reporter closed the door slowly, as if afraid of waking the typewriter, but its keys were waiting for someone else, and they slept on, safe and still in their metal casket.

Isham had a military car waiting outside the house. He wished Kant good luck in his search, and asked him to visit his office the next time he was in Dublin Castle. Kant waited, watching the car lurch off down the street, before he doubled back and slipped into the boarding house doorway. He hung in the shadows. It began to snow lightly and the street cleared of traffic and pedestrians. He had the odd sensation of the snow constantly sniffing him out, finding him in gloomy corners and doorways. A few flakes planted themselves on his boots, marking their target, more swarmed over his coat, clinging to his hair. He looked up at the pattern of snowflakes rushing towards him, like the stricken face of a woman wanting to be saved, but melting away at the last minute.

The door tugged open behind him, letting in a flurry of flakes, and then slid shut again. He grew aware of the silence inside the house. Earlier, the thought had occurred to him that there might have been someone else inside, monitoring their movements, listening to their conversation. The sudden draught increased his suspicions. Gently, he slipped through the door into the hallway, catching a whiff of fresh candlewax. The rickety staircase was dark but he was convinced its shadows hid the presence of an eavesdropper. After a few moments, a silhouette appeared at the head of the stairs. Kant waited, watched it extend itself into the shape of a thin man carrying a briefcase. For a moment, it remained motionless. Kant leaned forward and the wooden floor creaked. The shadow slipped back into the darkness above.

'Who's there?' he shouted.

A small sound echoed from above, that might have been a door handle clicking or a revolver setting. Kant climbed the stairs slowly. He explored the rooms on the landing above, each of them dusty and identically furnished. In the fourth room the curtains were drawn. Kant made out an extra shape in the darkness that shifted slightly when the floorboards took his weight.

'I know you're there,' he said. 'Identify yourself.'

'I beg your pardon.' A figure walked out of the darkness.

The stranger's politeness did not appease Kant, who felt a cold prickling sensation running down his spine.

'I did not mean to alarm you.'

'Then why are you creeping around like an intruder?'

A pale rumpled-looking man emerged fully from the shadows, carrying a thin briefcase. All the sinews of his body seemed to be holding onto the case as though it contained his entire life, which could not have amounted to very much. At first, Kant thought he was some sort of beggar. Empty boarding houses attracted all sorts of tramps and runaways, petty thieves and chronic drunkards, and this seemed to be the season for bumping into social misfits.

'I've been waiting for a visitor like you,' said the man in a whisper. 'Tell me, what happened to Lily? Why did she stop making her lunchtime appointments?'

'What do you know about her?'

'Practically nothing, I'm afraid.' He sucked his teeth in disappointment. 'You see, she was Mick Collins' girl. None of my business at all, but I had an attachment to the papers she'd been typing downstairs. I wanted them for my little collection. I've been working hard to fill this briefcase.' He squeezed his case, nursing it, the slender contents the sum total of his labours, and it, in turn, looked as though it were drawing all the life from him.

'What sort of attachment?'

'A very personal one.' His voice grew excited. 'What I would call my private little war with Mick Collins. I've searched the room below. The sanctum sanctorum. That Cork gallivant was running a very unusual operation in there. One that gave him a secret door to Dublin Castle's intelligence archives. A door he could enter and leave at will.'

'Blackmail and kidnap are dangerous games for a rebel leader.'

'Bloody dangerous games, I would say. Games the IRA never played until Collins took over the intelligence department.'

'You'd better tell me who you are.'

'My name is Cathal Brugha, Minister of Defence for the Irish Republican Army.'

'Then Collins is your comrade,' said Kant. He had heard of Brugha, or rather Charles Burgess, as he was called before joining Sinn Fein.

'His comrade? I very much doubt that.' Brugha's mouth twisted into a bloodless smile. 'I would say I am his most dangerous enemy, since I know the rascal better than anyone else. You see, I have made him my special field of study.' He tightened his grip on the suitcase. 'I know what makes him tick, his secret foibles and flaws. In fact, I'm the major obstacle in his path. The one person who has worked out what he is really up to.'

'Which is what?'

Brugha hesitated. 'I'm an amateur, Mr Kant. Not a professional reporter like you. For now, I am collecting routine observations, impressions, throwaway notes, bookies' debts, bar and clothing expenses, while Mick is busy protecting his official history, getting rid of loose-ends, tidying up his financial accounts, eliminating anyone who knows too much. Which is why I find it suspicious that this woman has gone missing. Of course, a corpse would be more inconvenient for Mick, if he's trying to cover up something discreditable.'

What exactly was he talking about, wondered Kant.

'A crumpled up receipt or a torn letter are only pieces of litter,' said Brugha, 'until someone wants them. Then they're intelligence.' There was something smug and dangerously delusional about the light in his eyes.

'I'm trying to find a missing woman,' said Kant, 'not ruin the political career of Mick Collins or change the course of Irish history. I want to find out if Collins has murdered this woman. If you're agreeable, I'd like to take a look in your briefcase, and see what sort of intelligence you've gathered.'

The leather handle of the briefcase creaked as Brugha tightened his grip. 'My notes are completely disorganised. I've yet to type and annotate them.' A grumbling tone entered his voice. 'I don't have Mick's resources, the team of secretaries with typewriters and reams of paper.'

'If you're trying to stop Collins, typing them is the least of your worries.'

Brugha backed away towards the door. 'I'm keeping this collection for a higher authority, an international commission that will be set up after the IRA has won this war. Mick will have to account for every penny spent and all his bloodthirsty acts.'

He held out a pale hand and Kant shook it.

'I wish you luck in your search for your missing secretary,' said Brugha. 'I hope you uncover the full extent of Mick's culpability in her disappearance, and that we will find some mutually acceptable way to work together in the future. For her sake, I pray that your search does not end with a corpse.'

He slipped down the stairs and disappeared into the street, where the snow was now falling heavily, like arrows taking aim at an ever-moving target.

FIVE

The boarding house where Merrin had been lodging was just three tram stops from Dublin Castle. The building looked shabby, but still held relics of its former glory, fanlights above the front door, wrought iron in the staircase, leaded glass in the windows. The landlady poked a thin, beakish nose at Kant's reporter's card, reading it carefully. Her eyes lit up with calculation when he mentioned Merrin's name.

She took in his slight stoop, the fact he was leaning on his cane and slightly out of breath. Melting snow pooled around his boots. 'This must be bad news,' she said. 'You've come to tell me she's dead.'

'No, not at all.' He didn't flinch under her searching gaze. 'I'm gathering information for a report in the *Daily Mirror* on her disappearance.'

'What kind of information?' She seemed determined not to give anything away without getting something in return.

'Just routine stuff. The type of woman she was. What visitors she had. Any contact with her family. That sort of thing.'

She looked at him shrewdly. 'I don't bother prying into my tenants' lives. Not during troubled times like these. Stick your nose in other people's affairs and God knows what they might stick in you. Besides, you're a reporter. What details I give you will be turned into a front-page scandal.'

'I want to lay rumours to rest. Not encourage conjecture.'

As was his habit, he stood on the doorstep to convey the impression that he wasn't going anywhere.

'This time of day I'm normally on my way to mass.'

He saw her hesitate. 'I won't take much of your time.'

'I never saw much of her,' she said. 'I really can't tell you how she'd been or what sort of woman she was.'

'Then let me have a quick check of her room.'

Fortunately, for Kant, her curiosity was stronger than her piety. More in an effort to convince herself, she remarked, 'I don't see why not. You're not the first visitor to tramp through her room these past few days.'

She led him up the stairs where a smell of ashes mingled with lavender. Kant's senses sharpened.

'Lily was a very quiet girl,' said the landlady. 'Kept herself to herself. Never had any gentleman visitors. Unlike some of the other girls.'

He could barely keep the anticipation from showing in his face when she took out a brass key and slid it into a door on the first floor. After some jerking, the door creaked open. The curtains had been pulled in the room within, and the smell of ashes grew stronger. His emotions were stirred by the thin line of winter light that crept under the curtains, a response anchored in his memory of the hushed hansom cab, and for an aching moment, he imagined the darkness might contain her presence. Something soft and light brushed against his hands, the gauzy material of a nightgown, he thought, but then it disintegrated at his touch.

The landlady opened the curtains, revealing a ransacked room filled with falling ashes. The draught from the door had disturbed them from an overflowing fire-grate. She opened a window to let in fresh air. A cold wind billowed through the curtains lifting another cloud of ashes from the grate. A muffled hush descended. They stood like grey trespassers, listening to Merrin's absence, the sound of ashes settling back to a floor covered with clothing and her personal belongings. There was only one thought going through Kant's head: Dublin Castle and I are not the only ones on her trail.

'Who else has visited the room?' he asked, trying to keep the tension from showing in his face and voice.

'Some men from the Dublin Life Assurance Company called a few days ago. They said she had worked for them and still had files in her keep.'

'Did they take anything with them?'

'I didn't search them, if that's what you mean.'

'But later, after they had left, did you notice anything missing?'

She stared at him in suspicious silence. 'How would I know what was missing or not? What sort of landlady do you take me for?'

'I meant no offence. Under the circumstance, it would have been quite normal, if you thought Mrs Merrin wasn't going to return...'

She shrugged. 'They left empty-handed. As far as I could tell. Anything they didn't remove went up in smoke.'

'What do you mean?'

'They burned a pile of papers in the grate. Left ashes everywhere. On the carpet. Even under the bed. It's a miracle they didn't set light to the chimney and turn us all to cinders.'

He bent over the fireplace and sifted through the remnants of the fire with his cane. Loose layers of scorched paper disintegrated at his touch. He picked out a few scrawled letters and numbers written in a precise, light hand. He leaned closer, feeling on the brink of a revelation, trying to trace the pattern of this slender thread of ink but unfortunately, he could make out nothing intelligible. The cold ash rose in his face, another veil hiding Merrin and her secrets. He remembered her hungry kiss and caress, the lure that had brought him to this rummaged through room. He tried to fix them in his memory, worried that they too might slip away, but his thoughts were as clumsy as his touch. He felt conscious only of her absence.

'Did she ever mention her son? An eight-year-old boy called Isaac.'

'She had a child? Now there's a surprise. I never even knew she was married. But then she didn't speak about her private life. Was told nothing so I know nothing.'

When the landlady left, he sat very quietly in the seat by the dressing table and tried to let Lily speak through the disarrayed objects of her room, the upended drawers, the smell of lavender soap mingled with soot, the nest of blankets, the glint of a blackened jewellery box full of paste necklaces, and in the wardrobe enough personal belongings to pack in a single suitcase. No evidence at all of family life, or that she had been someone's mother. It was like staring into a badly cracked mirror. All he saw were fragments, jarring insights into the life of a woman he knew only by her lips and blind fingers, and the messy handwriting of her son. He became aware of a clock in the landing ticking.

At least, he knew why General Stapleton was so interested in her disappearance. It had seemed a trifling matter searching for a missing secretary when the rest of Dublin Castle was chasing a rebel leader and his squad of murderers. Looking around the anonymous room, he had the feeling that its contents were decoys, and that Lily Merrin had been her own secret. Any clues to her family life had disappeared along with her.

Kant knew that some of the IRA's boldest operations were carried out by women like Lily who went to work every morning dressed in their ordinary work clothes. Spies who did not need cover stories, women in secret roles not even the leaders of the Republican movement were fully aware of, at least not their real names and the positions they held.

He stepped down the dark stairs, hearing the shuffle of the landlady's feet approaching from a room below.

At the front door, she shouted after him.

'Any chance of her coming back? Rent's due on Monday.'

'I doubt if you'll ever see her again,' said Kant.

He was beginning to understand that Lily's trick was like Collins'. To disappear from view, you had to make your life as transparent as the air you breathed.

Back in his boarding house room, Kant waited until the other lodgers had retired to bed. He locked the shutters of the windows and made sure the key was turned in his door. He sat on the edge of his bed and stared at the locked door, preoccupied with the tantalising daydream of Merrin's accidental kiss. He tried not to think about that afternoon and pushed the memory away, but his thoughts kept returning to the softness of her touch.

His brow furrowed with the burden of remembering what had happened after the kiss, Merrin's recoil when she realised he was a stranger, the fear knotting her face, the sound of a gun-shot and the rattle of the carriage pulling off at speed. He tried to remember the rest of their journey but his mind floated into emptiness.

If Kant had been asked to explain how important this gap in his memory was, to express it in terms of time, or recall what exactly had transpired that afternoon, he would have been at a loss to answer. He suspected that even the most gruelling of interrogations in Dublin Castle would not have drawn from him the precise thread of events. The most difficult thing to work out was whether the cab journey had been a dream or not. His body had felt paralysed, his senses numbed, but his eyes must have been wide open, his mind alert and conscious. He was sure of that. He remembered the horses straining at the reins, Merrin scrabbling at the door handle, he leaning back to give her more room, the carriage shaking, the glare of winter light through the window. Had she tried to open the window and climb out? What had she shouted at the driver? He could not remember exactly. It was as if her kiss had blinded him. And he had accepted the darkness like a gift. He did not want to give up the intimacy of that hushed cab, the softness of her lips, the touch of her fingers. He tried to pull his mind away from their first moments together, but his thoughts resisted his best efforts.

He saw the rest of that afternoon in snapshot pictures, snatches of disconnected conversation, jarring sensations; the way people who haven't slept for a long time remember an event, unable to force their thoughts to coalesce into a coherent whole. 'Who sent you?' He remembered her asking. He didn't know if he had murmured the truth or only thought it. His lips had moved and he had been unable to resist her interrogation. His hands had wanted to move too, but thankfully, he had been able to stop them, controlling them by tightly gripping his walking-cane. She had asked him about people he did not know. She believed he knew a lot more than he really did. He had tried to reassure her.

'I know nothing about who it is you are running from, that I swear,' he said.

'But if you did know something, you wouldn't tell.'

'I promise you with my life.'

He remembered her leaning back against the door and removing a leather-bound file from her coat. She clutched it to her chest.

He had wanted to tell her more, but was worried how she might react. He had been afraid to move or stir in any way. The carriage felt as though it was gaining in speed. Was the driver picking up the pace because they were being chased through the streets?

'I've spent too long carrying these secrets,' she'd said. 'Do you know why I stole the file?'

'Not at all.'

'Then you must hold onto it for me.'

These were the last words, the final image he could recall of her. He forced himself to remember more. He ransacked his mind but failed to summon anything further. His eyes were wide open in the cab and the file was in his hands, but she was no longer there.

He leaned back on his bed and closed his eyes. He was tired. His breath tightened and he felt the return of the familiar chest pain. He would have welcomed the dark immersion of sleep but his mind was too active, the ache in his chest too stubborn. He rose from his bed. Using a chair, he opened a trapdoor in the ceiling and slid from the darkness Merrin's leather bound file. The damp air of the attic had swollen its size. He untied the cover and carefully lifted out the pages. He laid them on his bed and studied the rows of numbers and dates. He tried to work out what Dublin Castle had found interesting about them, and why

Mick Collins was so eager to have them back. He was able to track some of the figures, sums of money paid to an Italian furniture maker, a further amount for shipping the goods, payments to harbour men that might have been bribes, the entire operation looking very like a gun-smuggling operation.

Money and war, he thought. The rebels and the banks shaping a new Ireland. Trade and power, a world far removed from the hushed hansom cab and the harried woman who had given him the file in the first place. Where was she now? He fervently hoped that she had not become another victim of this country's painful history.

SIX

The pine forest lay before the horseman and his companion, impenetrably dark against the whiteness. It had just stopped snowing and the laden trees were brimming with an icy stillness. The horse, a grey mare, swung too close to the branches, setting off ripple-effect cascades of falling snow, which the man walking had to skip sideways to avoid. The rider steered the horse deeper into the trees, making his companion curse. It was getting darker and the only habitation for miles was the nearby mansion Park House, from which they could hear the frenzied baying of hounds.

'Why meet here?' complained Thornton, who was on foot. 'You're not planning a picnic in the snow?'

'I enjoy the twilight,' replied Isham. 'The way the light lingers through the winter trees. It almost makes me sentimental.' He ducked his head to avoid the overhanging branches.

'Those bloody hounds. They're giving me the creeps.'

'I've ordered the groom not to feed them at the weekend. Keeps their appetites sharp for the hunt.'

Thornton trudged unhappily alongside the corporal, slipping deeper and deeper in the fresh snow.

'I need new boots,' he complained. 'This is a terrible winter. I need something with a lining to keep out the cold.'

Isham knew Thornton's type well. A veteran of the

Great War but at heart a rough-and-tumble street thug, an opportunist always looking for a hand-out. After being demobbed in 1918, Thornton might have easily joined the shadowy swarms of pickpockets and petty swindlers on the streets of London, but like hundreds of others, had boarded the first boat to Dublin. There was a hierarchy in spying, as in everything, and Thornton belonged to the lowest levels. Isham could see it in his constant uneasiness, the mix of fear and dependency that ran through all his relationships, even with the enemy.

They followed the path through the forest with its twists and turns, skirting the heavier branches, which constantly threatened to inundate Thornton with fresh snow.

'What progress have you made searching for Collins?' asked Isham. 'You've been dropping hints that you have good news for me.'

Thornton's eyes shone in the dim light.

'Progress, yes. I've discovered he's operating under the alias of a business man called Jack McAleer.'

'What sort of business man?'

'One with numerous bank accounts and offices dotted about the city. His headquarters are on Leeson Street. A secret office that can only be accessed through a hidden door in the Dublin Life Assurance building.'

'Forgive me for being sceptical.'

'About the existence of McAleer?'

'I'm highly sceptical about McAleer,' said Isham dryly, 'but at this stage I'm even more sceptical about the existence of Collins.'

Thornton's voice grew insistent. 'I broke into the Dublin Life building last night. I've checked out all the rooms. There was a secret passageway leading to the office.'

'You're sure it's Collins' lair?'

'I'm convinced. I've watched his bodyguards come and go during the day. And women carrying parcels.'

'Who are the women?'

'I don't know. They could be anything. His spies, his secretaries, his lovers.'

'What did you find in the office? Any guns or ammunition?'

'Just paper. Reams and reams of it. That's all he keeps there. Files of pages detailing the IRA's funds, the buying of weapons, payments to volunteers and their families, investments, travel and living expenses, even details of their secret bank accounts, all signed in his name.'

'What about his current whereabouts?'

Thornton grinned. 'We're in luck. I found a diary, detailing his meetings and appointments. He's due to visit the office tomorrow evening at 5 o'clock.'

Isham moved his horse on in silence, thinking carefully.

'Have you passed these details to anyone else?'

'No, sir.'

'Good man, Thornton. You will be rewarded for your discretion.'

In the distance, Isham heard the baying of the hounds grow louder. The groom was under strict instructions to keep them on a tight leash until he gave the signal. His throat grew dry with that special kind of anticipation that preceded a hunt. It was the expectation of a pleasure like no other.

'Stay close to me,' he murmured to Thornton.

He turned his mare back to Park House, and nudged the animal into a brisk walk. Thornton had to hurry to keep up. The increasing cold and darkness made the spy garrulous. He began talking at random about the freezing weather,

Collins' fondness for wearing business suits, his girlfriend's illness and that distant time when he fought in the bloodiest trenches at Passchendaele.

'If war broke out again, I'd like to go back to the trenches, sir,' he confided.

'What about the danger and the squalor?' Isham pulled up his horse. 'Don't you remember the agony of death? Why would one want to go back?'

'For the glory, sir.' There was a hungry, agitated look in the spy's eyes.

A flicker of annoyance ran through Isham. What did men like Thornton know about glory, apart from their selfish pursuit of ambition and notoriety? Glory was about military grandeur and that concept had been tarnished forever.

The spy gripped Isham's riding boot. His teeth were chattering. 'Tomorrow evening when we raid the Dublin Life building, I want your permission to shoot Collins.'

Isham urged his horse on, but Thornton held tight. The corporal felt something inside him recoil violently, as though the spy's hands were a dirty set of claws raking his innards.

'I'd like to be the man who rids England of her greatest enemy.' Thornton's voice was thick with spittle. 'I don't care about the bounty. All I want is a taste of the glory.'

'You know I can't grant you that.'

'Then I must act alone. This is my information, and I want the glory for it myself.'

Isham saw that he no longer had any choice in the matter. He stared at the spy's pinkish raw face, the Cockney eyes shining with a determined, dangerous light, the mouth that was almost drooling over his words. Isham lifted his whip in the air. The cold, rigid feeling in his body needed some form of expression.

'I'm sorry, Thornton, but I can't allow you to add your ugly little flourish to history.' He drove the whip across the spy's face. It was a practised, precise blow, lacerating Thornton's dark little eyes. The spy gave a surprised gulp as blood spattered over his face. The next strike dislodged his right eyeball, and left it dangling like a useless string of flesh. Isham kept raining down the blows upon Thornton's eyes, his expression blank, his breathing free and calm, as though he were well used to enacting such pitiless spasms of violence.

'The Great War is over, Thornton, but you're still stuck in the trenches. It's where men like you belong. Down there in the bottomless darkness with the rest of the cannon fodder.'

The blinded spy backed away, fingers groping over the red rags of his face, the heels of his hands pushing against the bloody mess. He tried to say something but all that came out was an animal-like howl. In panic, he veered into the trees. An aimless flight into deeper darkness.

'Where do you think you're going?' shouted Isham scornfully. He was no longer bored or cold inside. He raised a bugle to his lips and summoned the pack of hounds. The chase was about to begin.

A displacement of shadows at the top of the path announced the pack's arrival. They bounded in a long curve towards Isham, filling the forest air with their unruly baying. The corporal felt a stir of excitement in his loins as his horse reared up and faced the snarling, jumping hounds. His feet almost foundered in the stirrups, but he kept his balance, and drove his horse on, leading the pack towards their quarry. He caught glimpses of Thornton, his arms flailing as if he were swimming in the undergrowth, giving the hunt a delicious flavour of abandonment, like a Sunday jaunt at the beach. He wove his horse through the trees, fighting against the low branches, eager to keep up with the pack. He wanted to steep himself in the spy's terror, to ride deep into his blinkered panic. Thornton had spent most of his life peering suspiciously into the dark, now Isham was taking him beyond the limits of his normal vision, into his worst fears imaginable.

Even as the hounds leapt onto Thornton's torso, his hands were still clutching and scrabbling for survival, tearing themselves against thorn branches and the dogs' sharp teeth, fighting against the blindness that outraged his will to live. He fell into a thicket of elder, his face and heart and stomach opening to the seething hounds.

Isham waited awhile, circling his horse around the bloody scene. The sound of the rooks roosting helped drown out the spy's final screams. He felt no sense of wrong in organising Thornton's death in such a brutal way. That had been the spy's function. To accommodate whatever purpose his superiors required. And there was no purer purpose than sacrificing one's life for the schemes of one's betters.

SEVEN

The Dublin Life Assurance offices were situated in a nondescript building on Leeson Street, its solid façade of sooty brownstone fortified by stacked bags of sand and earth, an admission that sound financial planning was no proof against exploding bombs and trigger-happy troops.

Shortly before nine o'clock, Kant introduced himself at reception and was led by a secretary through a maze of filing cabinets to the account manager's office, a plate-glassed room occupied by a middle-aged man wearing rimless glasses called Dermot O'Shea.

'I came here early so as not to disturb your work, Mr O'Shea,' said Kant. 'I have an inquiry about one of your ex-employees. A woman called Lily Merrin.'

O'Shea looked up quickly from behind a stack of yellowing paper. 'What kind of inquiry?'

'I think you might be able to help me find out what happened to her.'

'Who sent you here? Dublin Castle?' His voice took on a weary tone. 'Is there no end to their snooping?'

Kant removed the reports of the missing women from his coat pocket and placed the sheaf in front of O'Shea. The manager read a few of the pages. A look of apprehension darkened his features.

'Why do you think an insurance firm might be able to help you?' he asked.

'Some men from this office visited Merrin's boarding house room a few days ago. I don't believe they were there by accident.'

O'Shea sighed and leaned back in his seat, letting the sheaf fall onto his untidy desk. 'This is a sensitive case, Mr Kant. We run a business here, but that doesn't stop us from using our own investigative services to protect our clients' interests. The woman you are looking for worked for the company a while back. She was in charge of some important financial documents, which have since gone missing. Understandably our clients have been breathing heavily on our necks, demanding their return.'

'Then you're not the only one anxious to find her.'

O'Shea's features grew lively with interest; his nostrils flared slightly. 'Do you know her whereabouts?' He glanced at the sheaf on his desk. 'We thought she might have ended up in hospital or prison.'

'She went missing a week ago. There's been no sign of her at work or at her boarding house. Dublin Castle suspects she was abducted.'

'What are they suggesting?'

'The file on your desk contains information on a number of missing women. In the past month, two of them have turned up dead in forests, their bodies naked and badly mutilated. I believe that Dublin Castle is trying to suppress the fact there's a lust murderer on the loose.'

O'Shea got up from his desk and stood at the window. He glanced back at Kant.

'None of us would know anything about violent death, Mr Kant, if it happened only once during our lifetimes.'

His shoulders drooped slightly and his eyes looked tired. 'In my capacity as manager of this life assurance firm, I think I have seen more brutal deaths than the general population of this city. Therefore, I must congratulate you, an outsider, for finding me here. You have come to the centre of things, the point where this city's inhumanity is at its darkest.' He waved a hand towards the distant view of Dublin's smoky terraces and slum tenements. 'I don't know if you can sense the fear and loathing out there. The ordinary citizens of Dublin don't know how the British soldiers will act from one moment to the next, and this puts them on constant edge.' His voice lowered to almost a murmur. 'It is the arbitrary nature of the violence that is most damaging. Checkpoints, reprisals, the scattershot rage that has soldiers burning entire terraces of housing. Then there is the violence against women. It appears to be the fetish of the hour. The physical assaults, the rapes, the drunken attacks with batons and whips.'

It was true, thought Kant. He had read the heavily censored reports about the behaviour of British soldiers. Sexual crime was undergoing a renaissance in Dublin city.

O'Shea stared at the file and looked thoughtful. 'This story about abducted women will carry weight. It will have an impact on the decent people of England if published in your paper. Are you determined to bring it to their attention, in spite of the danger?'

'Of course. That is my job. To report on what is there.'

'Ireland will have need of sympathetic journalists in the days to come.' O'Shea paused. He glanced at Kant anxiously. 'Perhaps I have talked more than I should.'

To Kant's ears, however, something more important was being withheld.

'My loyalty is to the company and our clients,' said O'Shea, returning to his desk. He reassumed his professional air. 'Their details should not be compromised. However, I feel that I can trust you, and our company owes some small debt to you for bringing this information. At the very least, we should tell you what we know about Lily Merrin. That responsibility lies with my boss, Mr McAleer. He will see you here at 5 o'clock this evening. He has some meetings to attend but he will have time to see you first.'

He shook hands with Kant.

'Be sure you come punctually,' he said, as the reporter left the room. 'Mr McAleer thinks it a sign of terrible manners to be late.'

Afterwards, Kant caught a tram back to the city centre. He walked up and down the streets, stared at posters advertising the latest plays in the local theatres, walked by the gates to Dublin Castle several times, but could not bring himself to enter its gloomy entrance tunnel. He waited for a long time on a bridge overlooking the Liffey. The river was rust-coloured and full of menacing potential, not like water, but something slower-moving, like blood, welling up thick with silted mud. He dragged himself away from the bridge and caught the stream of workers leaving their offices. He kept seeing Lily Merrin's stricken face dissolving into the unending stream of passers-by, into the shadows thrown up by packed trams rattling along the cobbled streets, into the mysterious light cast by boarding house rooms onto wintry streets.

For the past month, his daily existence had been like this. A complicated game of waiting, afternoon journeys on trams, days made up of pauses and blank spaces, all the time trying to come up with the connections, the people and the places that would bring him closer to achieving his mission. Over the past few days, he felt as though he were growing bodiless, like a ghost, haunted by this feeling of emptiness, his will to go on existing only within the memory of a single accidental kiss.

When it grew closer to his meeting with McAleer, he made his way back to Leeson Street. He walked along the shop fronts looking for somewhere warm to wait. He ordered a pot of tea and sat at the back of an empty cafe. He thought of his earlier conversation with O'Shea, the sense that he had hinted at something darker occurring at the life assurance offices. *'I must congratulate you, an outsider, for finding me here. You have come to the centre of things...'* He had the uncomfortable suspicion that he might be falling into some sort of trap. He stared through the café window at the pre-dusk sky, waiting, as his cup grew cold in his hands.

Two small ragged boys from the tenements stopped and peered through the glass. They had thick, dirty hair and wide eyes that seemed beyond fear or pain. They pointed at Kant as though he were some sort of aimless spirit, an object of pity. He buried his head in a newspaper, searching for headlines about other parts of the world, anything that might remove him momentarily from the watchful streets of Dublin.

When he looked up at the window, the boys had disappeared. A group of schoolchildren with a teacher entered the teashop, surrounding him with excited voices and the scraping back of chairs. He relaxed a little as the teacher, a young woman, ordered ice creams. He went back to reading his newspaper.

A draught of air carried a sweet, sophisticated scent to

his nostrils. The smell of cologne. He looked up. Two men had entered, removed their hats, and taken up the table by the door. The one with his back to Kant turned to speak to the waitress in a sharp English accent. He was surprised to recognise Isham's clean-shaven profile, his hair neatly parted, suit pressed stiff. He turned his attention to the corporal's tall, broad-shouldered companion. If anything, he was better dressed and more business-like in a city suit with a white shirt and smart cuffs that looked as though they could slice butter. He was talking to Isham with the self-important air of a man conducting business, a thick wave of brown hair falling over his forehead. Kant failed to place where he had seen his face before.

He was about to hail Isham when he remembered that no agent was permitted to acknowledge another while in the field. *'Show no sign of recognition that might jeopardise a secret mission'* was the instruction he had drilled into him. Instead, he listened through the noise of the children, making out snippets of their conversation. Isham's voice was almost unrecognisable. Flattered sounding and at the same time confiding. Through the gang of children, the reporter had an intermittent view of their table and the window beyond. Women rode by on bicycles with brown parcels in their bags. A terrier ran after them. The corporal pulled his seat closer to the table and poured his companion some tea. Kant had the feeling that Isham was playing a role, enjoying a situation over which he had complete control. He studied the other man's reactions. He noted that, although the big man's lips were grinning, his dark eyes were not. They glinted with intense wariness.

'Dublin Castle is watching the money,' he heard Isham say. 'They're chasing the money. They won't rest until they have blown your finances to kingdom come.'

'What can they do?' said his companion, shifting his shoulders slightly. He had a country brogue, soft and rising.

'Shut down your accounts for one thing. Then they'll go after the banks holding your money. They'll arrest the bank managers and close down their branches.'

'Then we'll just keep moving the money. Besides, a lot of it has already been converted into gold and hidden away.'

'No matter how many times you move it, British intelligence will follow every twist in its journey, every secret account.'

The big man moved uneasily in his seat. He opened a packet of cigarettes and lit one.

'When they find out how you've spent some of the money, they'll trumpet the news in all the newspapers,' said Isham. 'The rest of the world might stop feeling sorry for Ireland.'

The man examined the tip of his cigarette as if trying to divine guidance from the thin curl of smoke.

'My people at the life assurance office have become experts at moving and hiding money,' he said, his eyes glinting a little more fiercely. 'We've financed a shadow government, a prisoner's aid scheme and a guerrilla war with this complex network of cash. Do you think your bunch of civil servant snoopers is going to undo all this?'

The big man caught Kant's gaze. The reporter's eyes slid away and he picked up the newspaper again. He glanced back at the table to find the man staring straight at him, flashing a charming grin with just a hint of slyness. Something about his confident eyes, the easy smile and the lilting accent set off a memory like a flashbulb that almost jolted Kant out of his seat. The man bore an uncanny resemblance to Dublin Castle's smudged photographs of Mick Collins. Recognition must have shown in the reporter's face because the big man began to inspect him more closely. He buried his face in the newspaper, but he could tell that the man's head did not move, and that his eyes remained steadfast. The table grew silent. Kant felt the burning radiance of his interest prickle his scalp.

After a while, Kant glanced up and was relieved to see the two men had returned to their hushed conversation. He found it difficult to banish the reward posters for Collins' arrest and his photograph from his mind, the heavy fringe of brown hair, the sly, confident eyes, and Dublin Castle's assertion that he was the most wanted man in Europe. He tried to reassure himself that if the man were Collins, Isham must be playing some sort of covert role in the IRA's set-up. Another thought flashed through his mind. They had mentioned an assurance office. Did they mean the Dublin Life building? With all the mental concentration he bent to marshalling words for his newspaper reports, he tried to keep his thoughts clear, to swim through his rising anxiety. *'You have come to the centre of things...'* O'Shea's voice rang like a warning bell.

The door of the café opened. The two were leaving now, the big man laughing jovially with his hand on Isham's shoulder. They did not look behind at the reporter. Kant spent a while counting out the change in his pocket, then he paid his receipt and walked out. The sun was almost setting on the empty street; neither the English corporal nor the broad-shouldered Irishman were anywhere to be seen.

It was shortly after five, and he was late. He walked up the street, telling himself that the appointment with Mr McAleer had nothing to do with Isham's meeting in the café or their talk of hiding money. He was searching for a missing secretary, nothing else. Once again, the thought of Lily Merrin and her pretty face liberated warm feelings within him, the memory of her kiss filling him with a strange confidence, in spite of the growing tightness in his chest and the drumming of his heart. He remembered her anxious breath next to his ear, the tingling trace of her fingers, and the desperation of her twisting body. He was no longer the indifferent reporter hiding in a corner of a hansom cab, the spy weighed down by the aimlessness and apathy of fighting in a war that meant nothing to him. His imperative now was to ensure her safety, and his only available strategy was to let himself be carried towards the dark centre of things. The sense of moral urgency quickened his footsteps.

However, his optimism was cut short when he looked up at the life assurance building. The low winter sun blazed upon its glass, but he could still make out the shapes of two figures brooding behind the central window. One was O'Shea, the other, hanging a little back in the shadow, was the broad-shouldered man from the cafe. O'Shea raised his hand in greeting and smiled. Kant slowed his pace, his thoughts spinning in his head. It was too late now to change the course of his path, to turn back without arousing suspicion. Again, he tried to grasp the significance of Isham's meeting with the man he suspected was Collins, and the appointment that O'Shea had arranged for him. What if Isham were upstairs, too? What if the big man knew everything about his mission? Would Isham allow him to fall into a trap? Whatever the answers he had to continue as if he hadn't overheard the conversation in the café.

This was what it meant to be living in a city full of revolution, thought Kant. People swept along by chance encounters, the aimless and impatient pulled into the inner rings of dangerous plots, friends and enemies merging into a single stream. He gathered his will and mounted the steps. He glanced up at the window one last time; the golden evening light had deepened, filling the glass with a radiant darkness.

EIGHT

As soon as he pushed open the door of the Dublin Life building, Kant could hear footsteps running quickly down the stairs. He entered an empty reception, and a moment later O'Shea appeared, still wearing his friendly smile.

'I've allowed the staff to leave early, Mr Kant,' he said. 'The only people left in the building are here on appointment to see Mr McAleer. You've nothing to worry about in terms of secrecy.'

O'Shea accompanied him up to the first floor where he unlocked a narrow door that looked like a cupboard. He led the reporter along a dark side corridor, up a short flight of steps and into a gloomy waiting room. At first, Kant thought he was still in the Dublin Life building but a glance at the view from the window led him to believe otherwise. He was in another building entirely. He suspected that the side corridor was a secret passageway joining the two buildings, and that he had happened upon a secret office. O'Shea pulled out a seat and told him to wait for Mr McAleer's call. He disappeared back through the passageway.

Kant's eyes grew accustomed to the dim light and made out the shape of a figure waiting quietly beside him. He was surprised to see a man in a policeman's dark green uniform, staring grimly ahead. He could smell his sweat, sense the tension in his body, and was reminded of the soldiers dug in at the trenches on the Western Front, dreading the order to advance. They both waited, staring at the door in front of them.

'Mr Kant,' shouted a voice from the next room.

The reporter rose and opened the door. At the far end of a mahogany desk, silhouetted against the window, stood the broad-shouldered man from the café. Opened files covered his desk like a bureaucratic form of the card-game patience. Unlike O'Shea's office, the paper had not turned yellow with age. Instead, the pages looked freshly typed, sheathed in gleaming black covers.

The man motioned Kant to approach. 'My name is not Jack McAleer, Mr Kant, as I'm sure you've guessed already.' He spoke in a brusque but friendly tone. 'My name is Michael Collins, and you are most welcome to my paper fortress. Built of memos and minutes by an army of secret typists. Forget about bombs and guns. The real war of independence is being fought here on paper.' He thumped a stack of files emphatically.

'It's true,' said Kant, who was surprised he could find his own voice. 'Information is power. Facts, figures, propaganda…'

'Which is why my interest has been sparked by your reports.' Collins walked straight up to Kant, shook his hand and led him to a seat. 'With information like this we can grab the British by the throat.'

Kant glanced at the desk and saw freshly printed stacks of the Irish Volunteer handbook and heaps of pages outlining what appeared to be a food-rationing scheme. He also noticed a black revolver lying on top of a pile of green membership cards.

Collins sat down at the other end of the desk, lit a cigarette and gave Kant a quick grin.

'First, I want you to satisfy my curiosity. What gave you the idea in the first place; coming to Dublin and sticking your bloody English nose in our little war?'

Kant hesitated. Before he could continue, Collins pointed the burning end of his cigarette at him.

'I'm familiar with the lines you're going to feed me. I've heard them countless times.' He leaned forward aggressively but the tone of his voice was still good-natured. 'I've seen scores of men like you since the end of the Great War. God save us, but there are more of you every day. Showing up like worms. Some of you are rebelling against your upbringing and society in general. With your crudely formed notions of Irish nationhood, you think you can help shape our destiny, mould a piece of Ireland in your bare hands.' Kant shifted uncomfortably in his seat. 'On the other hand, there are those of you who come with less noble intentions. I have my informants at the docks paying close attention to all new arrivals. I know that the majority of you are more devils than angels. Come to sniff out my blood money.'

He paused and stared hard at Kant. His face looked magnified; the reporter could see every pore in his broad-jawed face, the thick wave of his brown hair, the lashes of his eyes, the inkblots of his pupils.

'I understand you have been asking questions about Lily Merrin. What has drawn you to this woman?'

'She has engaged my reporter's curiosity. I am concerned she might be the latest victim of a lust murderer. One who has already struck several times.'

Collins stood up behind his seat and gripped the backrest.

'My suspicions have been aroused because this is the wrong sort of story for you and your newspaper. Most of the women in your file were working for the IRA. Why should an English reporter and his readers care about rebel Irish women?'

'If a series of outrages have been committed against Irish women, then they will be.'

'England has grown war weary. I do not think its people are interested in what is happening here.'

'Then you underestimate the power of public opinion in your fight for independence. England won a war fighting against the oppression of smaller nations. Its civilians deserve to know if a crime has been committed in their name.'

Collins rested his cigarette on an ashtray. His face looked at once serene and fierce, and his eyes were firm, making it difficult to hold his gaze. Blue spirals of smoke wafted in the air.

'Are you a spy, Mr Kant? It would be better to tell me the truth now, rather than I find out myself later.'

'I'm a reporter working to finish a story,' Kant replied with a steady voice. 'Also, I have no wish to see more young women go missing or be murdered in this gruesome way.'

Collins relaxed a little and returned to his seat. 'Mr Kant, my war is completely dependent upon the careful documentation of information. In fact, I would say that information is the life-blood of my war.' He picked up the reporter's file. 'If that information is wrong or contaminated then it undermines my position and the legitimacy of my operations. Wrong information is more treacherous than a bullet aimed at my back. If I believe you have submitted wrong information in this report, I will have you shot. Make no mistake about that.'

'I can assure you that wrong information is just as treacherous to a reporter.'

'But how can I trust you? If you are the keen reporter you claim to be, you must be giving Dublin Castle a regular nightmare. They have an extensive network of spies. They ought to have gotten wind of you by now and deported you back to England.'

Kant chose his words carefully. 'My understanding is that British intelligence is trying to suppress the details of this case. They are sensitive to the value of propaganda.'

'Then you have been in touch with the enemy. You must tell me the truth. Who are you in this game of Dublin Castle's?'

'I've heard so much propaganda I'm not sure I know what the truth is myself.'

'Then let me tell you. The truth is what will hurt you.' He grabbed the revolver from the desk and walked over to the reporter. 'I have a simple proposal to save your life. Take my gun, walk out of this office, and shoot that bloody policeman sitting in the waiting room. Then I will know the truth.'

Kant did not move as Collins shoved the gun in his face. The IRA man's hard eyes shone with humour, as though the task might only be a jest to test the reporter's nerve.

'I tell you now I'm giving you this chance to gain my trust and save your life.'

Still the reporter did not flinch.

'Why do you hesitate? The policeman is an enemy of the Irish people. There is not a soul in this building who will stop you. All you have to do is use a little physical effort. Just pull the trigger and release.'

Kant took the gun and stared at it in his hand.

'What if the policeman doesn't deserve to die? What if he has a wife and five children?'

'He's a spy from Dublin Castle trying to dupe the IRA with useless information. I've grown tired of his countless attempts to entrap me.'

Kant's fingers twitched on the gun. He would never be in a better position to gain the confidence of the IRA leader, and prove that he could be trusted with the innermost secrets of the rebel organisation. He tried to summon enough courage to walk out into the waiting room and pull the trigger. But it wasn't courage he needed. It was hatred, a stubborn, pitiless hatred, and all he felt was sadness at the cheapness of life, its transitory nature, and sympathy for the policeman who did not come to the Dublin Life building to die.

'I thought there would be a purity and nobility in your fight for a new Ireland,' he said.

Collins gave an incredulous laugh. 'What made you think our war would be any different from other wars? Killing can only be combated by killing, and the end always justifies the means. I'm warning you now, if you don't use that gun, your inaction could lead to the death of several good Irishmen.'

'The policeman is no longer effective as a spy if you've blown his cover. Killing him will change nothing. Tell your men to ignore him and he will disappear.'

Collins stroked his hair across his forehead as if soothing a fever. He seemed to be running out of patience.

'Prove to me once and for all that you're not a spy,' he growled. 'And use the gun as I ordered.'

Kant pointed the revolver at Collins. His fingers tightened

on the weapon. It was the only way he was going to leave the room alive.

'My enemy is not the policeman but violence,' he said. 'Violence that has become an end to itself. Especially violence against women.'

Collins appeared not to notice that Kant was taking aim. His eyes were still hard, but they were no longer staring at the reporter. He was gazing beyond the reporter at some private domain. To Kant's surprise, Collins' jaw trembled and water welled up in his eyes. He lowered the weapon and waited. Several moments passed in silence, and then the IRA leader stood bolt upright, his eyes bold and clear again.

'What's that noise?' he whispered. A lorry rumbled in the street and screeched to a halt.

Before Kant could answer, Collins had grabbed the gun from him and flung open the door. The waiting room was empty, the policeman gone. Rough voices rose from the street below, soldiers' voices shouting out orders.

'We're being raided,' said Collins, his eyes shining with excitement. 'Do you think they're searching for you?'

'Most likely they're after you,' suggested Kant.

'Not necessarily. Your list of missing women will have made you a marked man.'

They could hear the sound of soldiers hammering on the doors of the life assurance building.

'Come with me,' said Collins. 'We'll slip out the back exit.'

'If they're after you, they'll have the back covered.'

'That's a risk we'll have to take.'

They ran down a passageway and climbed through a window onto a low roof. Collins pushed Kant first towards the edge, but the reporter baulked.

'What's wrong? Do you want to hang, man?'

Kant took a deep breath and leapt to the alleyway below.

Dim figures joined them in the darkness, Mick's bodyguards, or the Squad, to give them their popular title. Young men wearing hats and sharp suits, more like jockeys, than gunmen. They took off in a group and ran parallel to Leeson Street. They came out into a throng of shoppers heading home, women hurrying with heads down, shoulders hunched, carrying brown paper parcels. Mick grabbed a young woman's elbow and handed her his gun and Kant's report.

'Take these to O'Neill's bar on Grafton Street. Tell them Mick Collins sent you.'

Without a moment's hesitation, the young woman hid them under her coat.

Collins guided Kant onto a passing tram. Riding on the footplate of the tram were two of Mick's bodyguards, he could see them up-close through the glass, their thin, seamed faces, floating behind them like malevolent angels. He wondered where they were taking him to, but such was Collins' smiling good humour that he did not feel alarmed. The tram rattled along the cobbled streets until a view of Dublin port swung into view.

Kant looked into Collins' eyes, but could see nothing but plain good humour.

'You're a foreigner, Mr Kant. We mean you no bitterness but there is no profit in you remaining here. Go back to London and if you are sympathetic to our cause send us money and guns.'

It almost felt like a convivial farewell, until Collins leaned into him and hissed in his ear. 'Stop smiling. I mean to have you shot if I ever see you again.'

At the docks, they ushered him down the gangway and onto the mail boat. The final image he had was of Collins watching him from the dockside, smiling like a cherub, as the boat pulled off into the Irish Sea.

NINE

Prison had made her lovelier, exaggerated the darkness of her eyes, the vulnerability of her mouth. Isham had been secretly watching her in the cell for weeks, and had grown obsessed with this pretty brunette, who had flouted all the rules of her middle-class upbringing and renounced so much in joining the female brigade of the IRA. Perhaps she had grown a bit too thin in prison for Isham's liking, but that could not be helped. She was determined to sacrifice everything for the Republican cause and Mick Collins, even her health, and had barely eaten in the past few days.

Through the peephole, he admired her trim figure and the paleness of her skin. When she sat by the barred window in the afternoon, her hair seemed to grow candescent in the sunlight. She was young and enraptured and that made her irresistible to him. Amid the brutal, clanging cells, she was as strange and conspicuous as a white mouse among rats, and just as doomed.

He doubted that she would survive much longer in such a harsh environment, which was why he decided to spring into action that morning. Into her cell, he slipped a note telling her that Mick Collins had arranged for a sympathetic guard to leave her cell door unlocked during the 6 o'clock Angelus, and that she was to make her escape to the outer wall of Dublin Castle, where Mick and his men would be waiting for her.

Unfortunately, the guard on duty was new and had expressed his misgivings about Isham's plans.

'How can it be lawful to release a convicted gun-runner back onto the streets?'

'Who is going to release her?' asked Isham. 'No one. She will leave by herself. All you have to do is look the other way while the bells ring out this evening.' He tightened his lips into what was intended as a smile.

'But I am responsible for her custody, for the safety of the Dublin public.'

'Don't you understand? She will lead me to someone who is a far greater danger to public safety.'

'Mick Collins?'

'Correct. Of course, there will be a share in the reward money if my plan works out.'

The guard's hesitation had irritated him. But fortunately, everything had gone according to plan, and he was waiting for her when she stepped towards the side gates of the Castle.

She looked up at him in expectation and seemed disappointed when she saw his face.

'Were you expecting Mick?' he asked.

She raised her chin in an expression of defiance. 'Yes. Who are you?'

'A friend. Mick sent me to help you escape.'

She faltered a little, and took several steps back.

'What friend of Mick's speaks with an English accent?'

He stared at her pretty face, her blue eyes. He could sense her disappointment and fear. She must have been looking forward to meeting Mick. She had already given up so much in his name. Like the other members of the female brigade, she had probably staved off relationships with men, postponed her education, turned down job offers, clinging to her oath of allegiance to the IRA, while her peers excitedly discussed make-up, the latest dresses and dance invitations. She had already proved her worth to the cause. The gun-running charge she had been convicted of was as dangerous and brave as anything the male prisoners in the castle cells had committed.

'Don't be afraid. Mick apologises for not being able to come.'

Warily, she looked him up and down.

'Mick says it's too risky for you to return to the safe house,' he explained. 'They're expecting a police raid.' He hailed a hansom cab.

'Why should I trust you?' she said. 'You could be a double-crosser, an agent sent to gain my confidence.'

'I told you I'm an ally of Mick's.' The cab swung up beside them. 'Jump in and I'll take you straight to him.'

'Then prove it. Where does he keep his offices?'

'Next door to the Life Assurance building on Leeson Street.'

'Thank you.' She looked relieved. However, she was still reluctant to climb in. 'Where did you say Mick was?'

'I didn't.' He took out a pack of cigarettes. 'Would you like one?'

'Oh God, yes.' She took one and glanced up at his eyes.

'You can relax now.' He lit her cigarette. 'You're safe. Have you met Mick before?'

'Once.' She exhaled and gave him a grateful smile. 'But it was at a meeting. There were too many there for me to even shake his hand.'

He was touched by the desire in her face. But when she stared up at him with those burning eyes, it was not him she saw.

'Have you eaten recently? You look famished with hunger.'

'I've been living on prison rations for the past month.'

'Mick suggested we should get something to eat first. There's a tea-shop not far from here.'

She took another drag and nodded. He opened the door and they climbed in. Ten minutes later, they alighted onto a well-lit street, and entered a tea-shop, taking seats by the door. He ordered her some soup and bread.

'Eat up, you're far too thin.'

She coughed.

'We don't want you getting sick.'

She took several sips of the soup. 'You still haven't told me where Mick is.'

'He's having one of his naps. He was up all night writing letters and notes in those little black books of his.'

She smiled. 'What's he writing?'

'Some kind of diary. A defence of himself. An explanation of his movements. He also writes secret letters to women up and down the country. Women, like you, crying out to be rescued.'

'Has he written one for me?'

'He didn't give me anything so he mustn't have.' He saw the disappointment in her eyes. 'Perhaps he forgot.'

She returned to sipping from the bowl.

'Would you die for him?'

There was no hesitation in her answer.

'For him and Ireland.'

'But you know that Mick loves no one but himself. He

takes all the love from the women he courts and gives nothing back in return.'

He moved his hand closer to hers.

'A man like me could love you in return.'

She flinched.

'Am I troubling you?'

'No. Not at all.'

'But I am right in saying that you are upset.'

She stared at him. He felt provoked by the look of coldness in her eyes. It was like a key turning in a lock. He had been enjoying their little conversation, her nervous gaze, and the happy feeling that she was within his control, but now that pleasant sense of power had been banished. She saw him as little more than an intermediary, a helpful figure, who might bring her closer to the true object of her desire. He brooded over his sense of loss. It had been foolish of him to take her to this tea-shop, to try to seduce her in such a public place. He glanced at his pocket watch and patted it with his hand. He gave her a reassuring glance.

'Well it's time we were off.'

She rose and followed him into the street. What trusting ignorance, he thought. What mindless vanity to believe that Collins had made these special arrangements for her. What lovesick blindness could lead her to think she was no longer in mortal danger? In spite of his scornful feelings, her aura of innocence was a more powerful allure than any physical attraction. Hurriedly, he beckoned a cab and gave the driver directions to a nearby estate.

In the darkness of the cab, she made no sort of sound or movement, and he deduced that she had fallen asleep. However, when he leaned closer, her body felt rigid, unyielding. So far, he had shown great control and composure, but now his body tensed. He sat and stared at her dim silhouette, like a creature about to pounce forward. Patience, he told himself, soon their night expedition would begin.

The cab drew quietly to a halt at a snow-covered gate. He nudged her and they stepped out. She was subdued. Every living thing is born with a potential store of fear, and he could sense hers now. All through her life, she had been holding onto this reservoir of fear, waiting for the right moment to expend it.

He opened the gate and waited for her. She moved away from him, a shiver running through her shoulders. He grew alert.

'What's wrong?' he asked. 'You want to go back to your old life, I suppose. You'd rather not meet Mick tonight. Perhaps you've grown afraid of the sacrifices ahead.'

'I am not afraid. There is no going back to my old life.'

The way ahead was empty, not a soul in sight.

'Let us take the path through the trees. It will be safer that way.'

He walked on briskly, and after a moment's hesitation, she caught up.

'I must thank you for taking me to Mick,' she said, a little breathlessly.

He nodded. This carelessness, her disregard for her safety, only served to increase his desire. For a moment, the audacity of what he was planning almost made him feel dizzy. She barely lifted her eyes, just followed his steps.

For the past six months, he had taken to postponing these expeditions as much as possible, stalking only the most perfect quarry. He no longer hunted as recklessly as he had done during the dark nights of the Great War, when he was able to move freely amid the brothels that sprang up in the towns bordering the French battlefields, his victims of any size or age, the fly-covered remnants of their bodies littering the forests along no-man's-land. It almost nauseated him now to think of the aimless direction of his lust, the boredom that had been induced by his gluttony, the senseless repetition of the killing, his head always throbbing with desire for his next victim. Nowadays, he liked to prolong the intervals between his hunts for as long as he could. He suppressed his desires for weeks on end, surviving only on glances and furtive kisses. He suffered an inner torment, but felt almost purified by his self-denial, like a carnivore forced to survive on roots and leaves.

However, true abstinence always proved unattainable, and his craving soon grew unbearable. Fortunately, the Irish constabulary were easy to elude, and his military commanders could not keep track of his every move. Dublin was full of spies and rebels, anarchists and criminals, and the dangers for adventurous-minded women were innumerable.

He smiled at his new victim, taking in the anxious stare of her blue eyes, the silvery gleam of her skin in the moonlight, feeling almost elated by the days of withheld pleasure, all those unformed possibilities. She had no idea of the turmoil he had undergone, waiting for this opportunity to be alone with her, no idea that she was the prize, the reward.

She began asking him more questions about Mick but he raised his hand.

They had stopped in the middle of a dell, the ring of trees

crowding out the moon, and the only light cast by the snow, the night shadows creeping all around them.

'I come here often,' he told her. 'I feel a calm I don't get anywhere else. I like to stare at the hollows and dips in the snow. The way the wind makes patterns, like waves in the sea.'

She grew silent, staring all around her.

'You know that the wind cares for no one,' he said. 'It does whatever it wants. Some of these hollows contain my secrets.'

'What sort of secrets?'

'They were the final resting places of your colleagues. I like to come here and stare at the contours in the way the moon stares at the waves in the sea.' He took out a riding whip and a hunting horn, a cold light glittering in his eyes. With the whip he pointed to a path through the trees. 'That was where my hounds chased Susan O'Brien. And over there in the thorn thicket is where poor Agatha Hughes ended up. They all belong to my little collection of conquests.'

'Why are you telling me this?' She backed away, watching him with fear expanding in her eyes.

'I know I won't regret sharing my secrets with you. None of the others have broken their silence yet. They were just like you, girls who had lost their footing in life.'

She veered to the left, making for the closest tree-cover. He raised the horn to his lips and blew a series of long notes. She turned to look at him one last time, her silent, ghostly face. Only the eyes seemed to cry out at him from their depths, and then she ran into the trees. Unfortunately for her, it was the same direction from which his groom had been instructed to release the hounds.

He caught up with the dogs just as they were launching

themselves at her, propelling her body deeper into the snow, her clothes in disarray. He listened to the medley of snarls and yelps, the ripping of teeth through clothes and flesh. The moon disappeared and the shadows wrapped their cloak around the dogs' frenzied feeding.

TEN

The rows of reporters, copy-boys and secretaries pivoted their heads and followed Kant as he made his way to the editor's room in the *Daily Mirror's* London offices. Returning their gazes, he saw the brazen curiosity in the faces of the up-and-coming reporters, and the cynical boredom in the long-serving hacks, the silent and lazy, whose greatest daily adventure consisted of finding the route home from their favourite watering-holes. What did they see in him, he wondered, the famous war reporter returned from a dangerous stint in Dublin? A Lazarus brought back from the dead, marching into the lion's den.

Kant had headed straight for the offices as soon as he disembarked from the train, anxious to write up his report as soon as possible. Normally, when he submitted his copy, the editor kept him stewing for an interminably long time, but on this occasion he was summoned almost immediately. McArthurs, the editor, was a large-headed Scot with an angry, bull-like face, his neck straining in his collar. When Kant entered his office, he lifted up the report and bellowed, 'What sort of Fenian pigshit is this?'

'That is the preliminary report of a much larger story,' replied Kant. 'It concerns the disappearance and grisly murder of a group of women, who went missing from Dublin Castle.'

McArthurs crumpled up the report and threw it in a metal bin. He stared at the reporter as though he wanted to do the same to him. There was a silence as Kant returned McArthurs' gaze. The editor was breathing heavily.

'I am appalled by your naivety,' he told Kant. A muscle fluttered in his cheek as he fought to control his annoyance.

'In what regard?'

'This is the report of a man who doesn't give a damn for the interests of our readers. Have you considered the impact it will have on our forces' morale in Dublin? News like this will alienate our advertisers, and our friends in Dublin Castle will be enraged to see themselves vilified in such a manner.'

'I think even our friends in Dublin will agree that if we are to engage in propaganda by news, then it is important that our coverage should appear complete and candid.'

'What do you mean?'

'Readers are discerning and often sceptical. If every story I write about Dublin Castle reeks of rectitude then some might suspect too white a picture is being presented.'

McArthurs gazed at Kant for several moments, as if for the first time taking in his pale, haggard features.

'On the other hand,' replied McArthurs, 'many of our readers want the enemy criticised as virulently as possible, rather than presented as a catalogue of victims.'

'But in this instance, ignoring the plight of these women might expose the paper as a propaganda machine. Think of the story as a bluff in poker, a sound investment for the future.'

The editor's wide brow knitted. 'You will have to rewrite the piece.'

'What changes do you propose?'

'Present the bare facts and nothing else, removing any reference to the negligence of the authorities. And in the future, remember to leave opinion and deduction to the Irish constabulary and to our readers out there, who will draw their own conclusions in the safety of their parlours and sitting rooms. Make sure that you list the crimes these women committed at the end of your report, and that they were found guilty of treason by a British court. Hopefully that will lessen the sting of the article.'

Kant nodded. He had no doubt that, for the more patriotic *Daily Mirror* readers, the inclusion of those details would completely remove any negative propaganda effect.

McArthurs countersigned his expenses sheet. 'Be careful, Kant. You are in a privileged position with our friends in Dublin Castle. The owners of the paper might come to regard your little excursions to Dublin as an expensive luxury, especially if you keep siding with the enemy.'

Kant nodded again.

'When do you plan to return?'

The question stopped him short. 'I'm not sure I know yet.'

'Why the uncertainty? Are you worried for your safety?'

Kant shrugged. 'The level of danger is greater than any I have experienced. Yet somehow it doesn't seem quite real.'

'How?'

'The war in Dublin feels muted. A game of shadows. At times, it feels more like an hallucination brought on by ill-health.'

McArthurs looked at him dubiously. 'See a doctor, Kant. And take time off to recuperate.'

Perhaps McArthurs was right, he thought afterwards. He should reorganise his life back in London, allow his fatigued body and mind to rest. He took his expenses cheque and lodged it at his bank. He was so frugal with his money that he was able to save almost all of his commission. He had denied himself any form of debauchery and gained in its stead the banality of a savings account, a burgeoning amount of money set aside for a rainy day. The thought depressed him slightly – as though the more funds he accrued the greater risk of rainy days in the future. He looked at the evening sky. It was utterly blank, like a pane of frosted glass.

He returned to his lodgings on Holborn Street. In his room, he was surprised to find that his pillows were gone, and the bed stripped of its blankets and mattress. Someone had sealed his clothes and personal belongings in boxes.

The landlady looked shocked at his return. 'We thought you were dead, Mr Kant,' she explained. 'We fumigated the room to prevent anything spreading.'

For a moment, he tasted what his future held for him. God save him, he thought, if this were the end that lay waiting. 'Yet my rent is still being paid every month,' he complained to her.

He began coughing. His gaunt appearance prompted her to fetch some soup and a hard brown mattress for the bed.

That night, as soon as he closed his eyes, his mind flooded with subterranean images of Dublin. They were a welcome relief from the spectre of his death, and he fastened onto them greedily. He saw the billowing, black ashes of Lily Merrin's boarding room, the noticeboard of newspaper clippings where she typed every afternoon, the ugly shadows of Dublin Castle, where spies gathered like night creatures, and the hushed carriage on the day he had kissed Merrin.

He remembered the vitality of her body, its impulsiveness. His mind glowed at the memory of her furtive embrace.

An excess of energy took hold of him, more than the muscular restlessness induced by insomnia. He sat up in bed. He was no longer sleepy at all. He weighed up the possibility of returning to Dublin. On the one hand, he had Collins' death threat, but on the other, he doubted there was much of a life left for him in London. He reminded himself that he was still alive, that he had a body and a functioning mind. He had seen Merrin's boarding room, and followed her steps through Dublin. In addition, he had the goodwill of Dublin Castle, and the support of his newspaper. Best of all, he had the memory of Merrin's caress and kiss, a chink of light, a crack in the doorway leading back to her.

He got up and began sorting through his possessions. He was relieved to see that nothing was missing. He chose two new suits and hats, and a set of identity papers made out in the name of Harold Greer. He folded the clothes carefully in his suitcase, and, the next morning, booked his passage back to Ireland. What lay waiting for him in Dublin was the most perfect form of love, one without hope or despair, one based solely on the fleeting memory of a woman who had disappeared without a trace.

ELEVEN

Mick Collins' secret office in Chester Street was little more than a dark cubby at the back of a busy bakery. He sauntered in at precisely 6 o'clock in the evening, dressed in his soft, grey business suit, and doffed his hat with its elegantly dented crown at the giggling girls preparing the dough. He leaned over the counter, dipped his fingers in the flour and ran them through his hair. With the air of a shop manager, he opened one of the disused ovens, and removed a file of correspondence and a well-oiled Beretta gun. Then he climbed a back staircase to an office so tiny it strained to accommodate his broad shoulders. The room smelled like his other hiding holes, redolent of trains and back streets, bad weather and stale pubs. He sat at the tiny desk and bolted down the steak and kidney pie that one of the girls had left out for him.

He squinted at the bundle of letters in the dim aura of gaslight. It had been a hard day of negotiation with the members of the shadow government over strategy and finances, and his mind was tired. He began with what he called his 'lovable letters', the ones from his devoted female followers. In reply, he wrote them hurried notes, sometimes slipping into the envelopes a little love token, a piece of ribbon or a boiled sweet.

He spent more time thinking of his response to the

letter he had kept until last. The woman who had penned the love note deeply stirred his feelings, but he exercised soldierly restraint on his emotions, and flooded his mind with the religious imagery that decorated the stained glass windows of his regular church. In his careful, civil servant's handwriting, he wrote, *'Was at two Masses today! One in my usual oratory 8 o'c. The other an official one at Maiden Lane. Even at the official one, I managed to come back and light a candle for you. Second one therefore, today.'*

He put down his pen. It had been a hard day for him. His mind moved from the incense-filled church to a more turbulent vision, an image of two mutilated girls lying face-up in the forest, snowflakes melting in the dark sockets of their eyes. He doubted if anyone had offered the dead volunteers a confession, the Last Rites, or any sign of grace. He was not sure how this appalling apparition had forced itself into his mind but all he could think was God help him if that was how his lover ever met her maker. He felt a strong need to close his eyes, and place his head in her lap, to have her stroke his hair and nurse his disorderly thoughts back to peace.

For a while, he made do with listening to the soothing sound of the bakery girls brushing the floors below. The place had been spotlessly clean when he entered. It seemed to be their favourite chore while he was in his office, sweeping back and forth across the stone-flagged floors in an unvarying rhythm, a routine he suspected helped keep their nerves under control.

With a sigh, he turned his attention to his official correspondence. Receipts for weapons he had to sign, gunmen's expenses to be logged and counted, the funding of his secret network of informers in Dublin Castle, and on the railway lines and ports. Then there were the begging letters to be answered, requests for financial assistance from injured combatants, prisoners' wives, widows with starving children, so many demands flooding in upon one man.

His brows pushed down harder upon his eyes. He remembered Isham's words of warning. *'Dublin Castle is following the money...'* He rubbed his cheeks until the bones beneath his flesh felt sore. His staff at the Dublin Life Assurance company had given the National Loan a dizzying financial history. They had created a financial mirror game where left was right and right was left, the money switching constantly from account to account, backwards and forwards, in and out of investments, making it virtually impossible to trace how it was spent, and in whose name. Now the crackpots in the IRA's ruling council wanted all the money to be traced, every penny he handed out accounted for. He shuddered at the book-keeping task that lay ahead of him. He was not even close to knowing where all the money had gone. There were IRA officers who showed up asking for funds to finance gun-smuggling manoeuvres that were aborted at the last minute. A degree of speculation was sometimes called for if a bomb-making operation was to bear fruit. There were just too many levels of plotting, too many operatives demanding cash for their schemes. Revolutions like the War of Independence succeeded because of daring plans and visionary leadership, not because of the bean-counting obsessions of bank-clerks. It annoyed him deeply that he had to keep the IRA's finances safe from the prying eyes of the British authorities, while at the same time protecting himself from any charges of misspending the money or manipulating the accounts.

After scribbling down several pages of calculations, he

grunted and angrily tore them up. 'To hell with them, they expect me to have a superhuman memory.'

He decided to write letters to every member of the ruling council outlining his predicament and an estimation of costs. So immersed was he in his paperwork and the secret financial landscape of the IRA funds that at first he did not notice the unusual silence that had descended on the bakery. His eyes were hard and bright with inner calculations. After a while, he paused, laid down his pen, and listened.

The girls had stopped sweeping the floors, which made him instantly alert. A moment later, he heard a sharp English voice issuing commands followed by the rumble of hurried boots and a series of soft explosions.

'Holy God, not another raid,' he cursed. Unfortunately, this time they had trapped him with no escape exit. A cloud of flour from a burst sack billowed up the stairs. He listened to the grunts and coughing fits of the soldiers. They were bayoneting the sacks, he realised, searching for hidden weapons and ammunition. Who had given them the tip-off? Puffs of flour fluttered through the office doorway. He grabbed his gun and, leaning round the lintel, stole a glance down the stairs. The soldiers were dusted from head to foot, flapping about like moths, burst sacks flailing around them. He wondered if the flour might blind them long enough to make a daring escape. A voice rapped out more orders and several of the coughing soldiers squirmed their way towards the back stairs. With surprising grace for his large frame, Collins stepped on his table, quickly heaved open the narrow skylight and pulled himself onto the roof.

It was cold and calm upon the moonlit tiles. He inched his way along them, disturbing the roost of a few bedraggled pigeons huddling together for warmth, until he was well beyond the light cast by the window. He heard a commotion erupt in his office below, and saw a white powdered face press itself against the pane of the skylight, and then another. He leaned into the shadow of a broad chimneystack. The skylight opened, and a soldier's pale and gloating face appeared, eyes rounded with effort, scanning the shadows on the roof. Then out popped his arms, feeling around the tiles for something to grip upon. With a grunt, he began heaving himself onto the tiles.

From a crouching position, Collins contorted his body, a movement demanded by the need to withdraw his gun. Unfortunately, he lost his balance; his body twisting further, arms whirling, head leaning back. At the last moment, his flailing hand caught a section of guttering. He gripped it with all his strength. It was enough to help him regain his poise. However, his gun had fallen from his inside pocket, skittering over the slates and falling with a nauseating clang onto the street below. The force of the impact triggered the firing mechanism, and a bullet ricocheted against the shop-fronts.

'Gunman on the street!' shouted an officer from below. An army lorry roared into life, and a volley of rifles answered the stray bullet. Something seemed to tug at the soldier's body in the skylight, and he disappeared from view. He heard the thunder of boots retreating down the stairs. He sank to his hunkers, murmuring a prayer of thanks.

After the soldiers had left, he waited motionless on the roof. After a while, it began to snow, the flakes forming a helmet of cold around his bare head, melting down his neck and into his clothes. When about an hour had passed, he slithered back along the roof, his body numb and sloth-like, and eased himself through the attic-window. He changed out of his business clothes, which felt as heavy as a sheet of lead, into sturdier, warmer clothing, a labourer's wool jacket and moleskin trousers. He slipped down the stairs, through the dust-filled bakery, and onto a side street where he had hidden his bicycle under a lump of tarpaulin.

He urged his stiff limbs into action, and cycled through the snow-covered streets, unsteadily at first and then picking up speed, past long, dejected-looking rows of shuttered shops and factories. A stray dog kept him company for several streets, panting to keep up with him, until he swung into Wicklow Street with its view of Dublin Castle rising above the commercial heart of the city. In daylight, he liked to wander close to the monument to Britain's colonisation of Ireland, so many secret plots and conspiracies converged within its fortified walls. Its limestone and brick towers were always jutting into his consciousness, even in his sleep. He braked and stood his bicycle in the centre of the street. He remained there for several minutes, contemplating the vision before him. The entire castle shimmered in the moonlight, like an oppressive dream of the past. Its odd jumble of building styles and materials dated back to the twelfth century, the crooked battlements interlocked by remnants of the ancient castle walls, the round towers resembling Norman fortifications that had been seized, roped and hauled from medieval Ireland and raised as trophies within the castle's modern walls. They reminded the population that Britain owned the country, past and present, its history and its future.

Pedalling on, Collins hurled his bicycle along the gas-lit streets, until the castle, melted back into the starry night. He grinned to himself. The British were like rabbits hiding in their hole, he thought. As holes went, Dublin Castle was adequately defended, but he knew that out here, in the real city, where his men were plotting in pubs and boarding houses, the entire order of British rule was collapsing like a set of rotten roof beams. Propelled by his good humour, he sang a few bars from an old rebel song, sprinkling the unmistakeable notes through the abandoned streets.

Soon he was at the outskirts of the city and cycling past the walled estates of landed gentry. Away from the street shadows and the ever-present threat of danger, he was able to think more clearly. He thought of the naïve English reporter who looked and sounded like a spy. Since his departure at Dublin port, Collins had run into several raids, managing to escape by his quick wit and good fortune. An uncomfortable feeling that his luck had changed, and that the British were tightening their net around him, played on his mind as he cycled further south.

After several miles, he hid his cycle in a ditch and made his way along a tree-lined avenue. The imposing shape of Furry Park mansion, the residence of republican sympathiser Moya Llewelyn Davies rose before him, wide as a military barracks. He ignored the warmth and hospitality the lady-of-the-house would have offered him, and skirted the estate grounds through a plantation of pines.

Eventually he emerged at a bleak stretch of coastline, a wilderness of marram grass and blowing sand hills. He followed a hidden path through the dunes to a little bay he had chosen especially for its secrecy, hidden from roads and passing traffic.

It was a windless night and the surf that usually roared across the bay had all but disappeared. It was soothing, all this expanse of sea, the slow-paced waves glittering in the moonlight, the distant horizon. He breathed in the salt air, filling his lungs deeply. The most fortunate people on earth were those who could be on their own long after the sun had set, he thought, who could be secretive about their whereabouts, who could let their fears and cravings subside into the silence of the night sky.

It had been weeks since he'd enjoyed such space and fresh air. A weight lifted from his chest, and for the first time in days, he realised how harassed his life had become. His revolution seemed at times nothing more than constant bureaucratic agitation, monotonous ink on paper, endless accounts and note taking, a series of quarrels and contrived alliances with men who had once been close friends. He had spent too long in the shadows of the insurance office building and grey boarding houses, he realised, dodging the army raids, and the wanted posters, that were now hanging like rags after months of bad weather.

He hopped from rock to rock, invigorated by the thought of the mission ahead. A squad of his men were smuggling ashore a weapons shipment, and something else, a personal consignment, not part of the larger war, not expendable like bullets or guns, a package so important he would have to lock it away in a secret room.

He found a suitable perch on a large rock, and surveyed the beach. A light winked on the other side of the bay. His men had lit a signal fire out of turf and gorse.

'Who goes there?' shouted a voice.

He replied by whistling a tune. Even his most nonchalant sounds these days were coded. Everything had its hidden meaning. He looked forward to the time when he no longer needed secret communications to get through his day.

He introduced himself by playfully lobbing a dead crab

at the shadowy figures. They were a flying column from the Wicklow Mountains, men used to sleeping rough in derelict cottages, and camping in forests. He had told them to lie low and speak to no one about the unusual task assigned to them. Collins wanted the entire mission wrapped in secrecy.

'You're looking forward to this, Mick,' said their leader, a middle-aged man in a dark fisherman's sweater with a woollen cap pulled low over his heavy brows.

'I am, indeed.'

'Here.' He passed a cigarette to Collins. His eyes glittered in the firelight.

'This is a new kind of danger you're getting us into Mick.' There was a warning note of displeasure in his voice.

Collins drew on his cigarette, exhaled and smiled broadly at him. A tension grew in the air. The other men glanced gingerly at his fathomless grin.

'How long must we look after the package? Hours, days?' asked the man.

'As long as it takes,' said Collins.

The sound of a chugging outboard engine floated above the wash of the waves. Their attention turned to the sea and the slight swaying of a lamp that marked the approach of a fishing boat. They made their way down to the shore and waited as a smaller rowing boat struck off towards the beach.

The waves picked up in a strengthening wind, thrusting the rowing boat towards the rocks. There were several rebuffs and much scuffling before the men on board were able to row into shallow water. Collins and his men waded in and secured the vessel with ropes so that it would behave itself while they unloaded the cargo. Collins led his men, stripped to his shirt, leaping in and out of the waves, hoisting the crates of rifles onto his shoulders, racing across the sand and pitching them onto a small cart that the flying column had hidden at the head of the beach. When they had added the last teetering layer, and covered it with fresh straw, Collins roped the load tight and sent the driver on his way.

The wind picked up again. The men's shirts flapped black and chill with the sea. The tension between Collins and the flying column returned. Some of them shuddered; they had one more load to lift from the boat.

The vessel had swung away, its weight lightened, the ropes loosened by the action of the waves. Collins splashed through the waves and drew its nose to shore. One of the men approached the stern, and lifted out a loose bundle, a small limp body wrapped in a thick blanket, head covered with a hood.

He stood the bundle on the sand, and it stiffened into life, making a little grunt as it found its feet. Collins removed the hood. The moon shone on a boy's sleepy face, hair matted and damp. The child took some moments to react to his new surroundings. His legs wobbled and he lurched forward. The men positioned themselves around him, uneasy, watching him adjust his stance. Pale sea spray filled the moonlit air, giving them all a dazed, blinking expression. The leader took out a knife and slashed the ropes securing the boat. He could have untied the knots and saved the rope, but he wanted Collins to see the knife. It was a signal, a gesture that he was reluctant to put into words. He ran the blade along his rough sleeve.

For several moments, the boy stood without moving, absorbed by the task of keeping his balance against the retreating waves. He seemed unable to get the attention of his feet. He stared around him. The sea where he had come from seemed less treacherous than this wild shoreline and the circle of shadowy men. For a moment, they all shared his stillness, wariness etched on their faces.

Collins put his hand on the boy's shoulder and coaxed him forward.

'Come on, Isaac, my boy. We've a bed in a warm cottage awaiting. You can sleep like a babe till morning and no harm will come to you.'

The boy made some tentative steps, and fell into line behind Collins and his squad.

'He'll get in the way,' warned the leader. 'How are we to feed and look after a child?'

'There's a woman coming down from Furry Park. She'll be a help.'

'Your hostage will make us hunted men. He'll remember our faces and our voices.'

Collins grinned, but he knew the man was correct. The boy's abduction had set in motion dangerous forces. Despite all his preparations, his meticulous planning, he knew Dublin Castle were on the boy's trail.

'Think of the child as business.' He waved his hand dismissively. 'A fine young calf you're taking to market. Weapons aren't the only things traded in war.'

They filed up the beach, through the plantation, towards a tiny cottage hidden amid the bushes. The young woman that Moya Llewelyn Davies had sent was waiting for them at the half-door. She ignored Collins and his men at first, focusing her efforts on the boy, correcting his stumbling movements, wrapping him in freshly warmed blankets, guiding him into a fire-lit side room.

The squad of men watched her reappear after several

minutes. She smoothed her skirt and stared candidly at Collins, her composed features communicating a shared secret. They stood together closely in silence. She reached up and touched his hair and his cheeks.

'You're covered in dust,' she said. She held up a cobwebby skein of flour, dampened by the sea.

Collins did not reply. He followed her into the side room.

'Women will be the death of Mick,' said the middle-aged man to his companions. 'It's shameful how our leader brings disgrace on himself chasing after these casual women.'

His eyes grew murky with the dregs of contempt and envy.

TWELVE

A strange terror overcame Kant in his sleep. He felt as though a blinding light was shining upon him, stripping away the comforting darkness of sleep, and then he saw the figure of a man striding out of the light, the steep-shouldered figure of Michael Collins, looking as though he had been marching for a week, with his right shoulder set forward, cleaving the air before him. He made no sign of slowing down; the grim face with its buoyant eyes sweeping up to Kant's bedside, its bottomless grin invading the reporter's deepest sleep.

He awoke, bleary-eyed, to find rough arms pinning him to his bed and a cold Cork voice whispering, 'Mr Kant, when something goes wrong I always blame an Englishman. You were the first I could think of.'

The arms released their hold and Kant sat bolt upright in bed, rapidly awakening as he took in the dim shapes of his early-morning intruders. Someone turned on the gas lamp, and shone the light in his face.

Michael Collins had changed since the last time they had met. More solid and extroverted, broad-shouldered as a bull. However, he was dressed in the same neat grey businessman's suit, while his henchmen in their double-breasted waistcoats and dapper outfits looked more like a bridal party still up from the night before.

Collins regarded Kant with a look of appreciation, which immediately darkened into suspicion.

'According to your landlady, you're registered under the name of Mr Greer. Why have you come back to hide in my city, Mr Kant? What trouble are you planning against me?'

Kant shrugged. 'The *Daily Mirror* sent me to report on your war. If I don't work, I'll starve.'

'A sensible man would have signed himself into a London poorhouse rather than come back to haunt me.'

Kant tried to swing himself out of bed but broke into a racking coughing fit. He wiped his mouth with a handkerchief, covering up the spots of blood.

'I have a duty to my employers that I must fulfil, plus I have an allegiance'. Kant swallowed thickly. Due to the pain in his chest, he struggled to remember the full details of his story. Another coughing fit spittled his handkerchief with blood. He stared at Collins' henchmen. A new expression formed on their faces.

'What are you staring at?' he asked.

'What sort of employer sends an invalid to war?' one of them asked Collins with a note of disgust in his voice.

'Don't you know that Dublin Castle is full of men with death-wishes like Mr Kant,' said Collins regarding the reporter with interest. 'A craving for one's own demise is a kind of madness in itself. I've seen it in men before. In poets and intellectuals, men like Padraig Pearse and Roger Casement. It's the most dangerous disease of them all.'

Kant lay back against his pillow, still as an animal trapped in a snare. Collins sat down at the edge of the bed, and removed a dark object from his pocket, something neat and practical. To Kant's relief it was a notebook, not a gun. All

Collins' energy and will seemed focused on the book, which he brushed with the tips of his fingers.

'I've told you before, Mr Kant. This war I have started is not just about guns and bullets. It's about the contents of notebooks like this one.' He leaned back and waggled the book in the reporter's face. 'It's about words and information, messages and codes. You see, I have devised for myself an extensive and secret bureaucracy. Everything is documented and analysed. Sometimes the burden of paperwork becomes unbearable, and I struggle to keep a sense of clarity, even though I have several teams of secretaries working for me. I listen carefully to every voice that reaches my ear and I write down every word I hear, but sometimes in the deluge of information, I am overwhelmed and make mistakes.'

He stood up abruptly, flashing Kant a lopsided grin. 'Which is why I was so attracted by your neat little report of missing women.' He paced up and down by the bed. 'However, I worry that your true purpose is to betray me. That you are trying to deceive me with your facts and figures.' He stepped into the middle of the floor to give himself more space. 'Since the British placed an enormous reward on my head, the streets of Dublin have filled with touts and cut-throats, a stranger gallery of characters you would not find in even the most sensationalist of your colleagues' imaginations. Believe me, I know, because I have had them all checked out by my men, every one of them, spies and adventurers on the make, fanatics and plain lunatics, thieves and murderers.'

As Collins spoke, Kant watched his men poke and pry through his private things. They rummaged through drawers of clothes, and thrust their arms under his bed, only stopping short of ripping open the floorboards. He said nothing, just breathed heavily.

Collins struck his chest with his fist. 'God damn it, if you weren't such a wretched creature, I'd wrestle you to the floor myself and squeeze the truth out of you.'

The men knocked over Kant's wardrobe, sending it crashing to the floor.

'You haven't told me on what grounds you suspect me of being a spy,' said Kant.

'On the grounds that you concocted the details of these disappearances in order to track me down.'

'Why should you entertain such a ludicrous thought?'

'These disappearances strike me now as strange. They never appeared in any other newspapers or in any police files. Not even in our own reports of atrocities.'

'It disturbed me also that the disappearance of these women did not seem to matter to anyone but their nearest relatives. Remember, I was the first to gather the reports for the whole of Dublin city. Your network of secret cells is only aware of volunteers missing within their own small circle of volunteers. No one had looked at the pattern of disappearance on a wider scale,' said Kant.

'All right, you've made your point. You discovered a pattern, a possible connection between these women. What concerns me more is the fact that an army raid interrupted our first meeting. The following day, another of my offices was searched while I was on the premises. And then an informer tells me that a British general has been boasting how his new Englishman managed to track me down in a matter of days.'

'You can't honestly believe that I am after your blood money.'

'What I believe and what's the truth may not be the same thing.'

Kant watched from the corner of an apprehensive eye as one of Collins' men studied the trapdoor in the ceiling. He had hidden Merrin's secret file of accounts there, and he knew that if they found it, his game was up. He caught the man's eye and glanced nervously at his bookcase. The squad member followed the surreptitious cue. He toppled the bookcase and began shovelling through the reporter's books and papers. The reporter averted his eyes from their brutal efforts. His innards convulsed as though they were poking his vital organs.

'Don't rip up my papers.'

The men hesitated for a moment, stared at him, and then promptly began ripping up the files, scattering the pages across the floor. Collins paced about, studying the scattered notes.

'I have an idea how to settle my suspicions,' said the IRA leader eventually. 'I plan to take you to my informer at Dublin Castle. He will be able to say whether you're in the pay of British intelligence or not. It shan't matter if you lie or tell the truth then.'

Kant wondered was he talking about Corporal Isham? For the first time he considered making a run for it, but before he could weigh up his chances, Collins' henchmen grabbed him by his shoulders and forced him to get dressed. Then they hauled him out of the bedroom and down the stairs.

'Come my intrepid reporter,' said Collins, 'we are going on a little trip together. I would advise you not to make a run for it. Remember you are walking a tightrope and I am the man holding the rope.'

Kant felt a cold terror settle in his gut. He had thought

consumption had mapped out his future and the manner of his death, but now he realised his life and death no longer belonged to him or the disease that he carried in his festering lungs.

THIRTEEN

They half-dragged, half-guided Kant towards the train station, the squad members barely exchanging a word, only staring straight in front, ignoring the reporter with his ruffled hair and flushed face as though he were some sort of drunken flunkey in their midst. The air was freezing cold, and took away whatever breath he had left in his lungs. Murky shadows gathered in the sky, not a nocturnal darkness, but the gloom of an approaching storm. Rain fell at first and then turned into a wet, stinging snow. Vagrants had lit fires in the streets next to the slum tenements, the smoke adding to the murk, sediments of ash and snowflakes colliding. It was hard to make out the blurred shapes of the squad members as they escorted him to the train station. To passers-by, they must have looked as sane and acceptable as everyone else hurrying under the trailing plumes of smoke and snow.

He had left without his overcoat or a hat, and he could feel a chill take hold. His legs ached and his mind felt like pulp. He tried to push his fear aside and concentrate on working out some sort of escape strategy. Every now and again, he thought he recognised a face in the crowd of pedestrians as they loomed out of the squall, but they were all strangers. If a man or a woman caught his gaze, they just stared blankly back, submerged in a gloom that made everything look grey and anonymous. Why should anyone care about his plight on a morning so full of impediments?

The platforms at the station were clogged with people waiting in queues. He thought of signalling one of the train guards but felt the cold jab of a gun in his side. The crowd rushed as one when a train entered the station and for a moment, he broke free from his captors. The push of people against him made him feel as though the battle was not yet lost. There was a blind safety in crowds, even one that concealed the movements of IRA assassins. He allowed the throng to jostle him further from Collins and his henchmen. He thought he had lost sight of them until he felt someone grip his shoulders tightly, and force him in the opposite direction, and then onto a train that was just about to depart.

Collins and his squad filed down the corridor, with the reporter in the middle, until they found an empty carriage. From where they made him sit, next to the carriage window, he could see the lever for the emergency stop but it was so far away that reaching it in one movement was out of the question. He turned to look outside as the train pulled away. All he could see were railway tracks gleaming in the falling snow, curving in places, changing direction and transecting each other, like a page crowded with lines of writing, the words wandering and slanting into each other. He stared through the window at the figures of people frozen in the moment but he was beyond their help. He shifted uncomfortably. The point of the gun nestling in his ribs felt like a cold prophecy of what the day ahead held.

At the next station, a slim, professorial-looking man dressed in a trilby hat and a fawn coat entered the compartment. Collins introduced him to Kant as Richard Mulcahy, his Chief of Staff. The reporter recalled that Mulcahy was a long-term friend of Collins, and a veteran of the 1916 rising in which he had been credited with defeating a Royal Irish Constabulary column.

The two men began firing questions at Kant, which he tried his best to parry. The morning's exertions had brought on a fever, and in his tired state, the regularity of the train's clacking on the tracks became a metaphor for the relentlessness of their questioning. The IRA men's voices and the shape of passing buildings came at him out of the darkness with a mechanical rhythm. Mulcahy had cold blue eyes, and his fingers traced invisible patterns in the air as he spoke, as though he was playing a game of noughts and crosses with himself. He spoke in a formal dry voice, while Collins adopted a jolly, kindlier tone.

'What sort of spy are you, Mr Kant?' asked Mulcahy.

For a moment, he felt as though he was back in his headmaster's study, confessing to a minor violation of some school rule that might lead to a reward of sorts. He was surprised by his own reply, the child-like truth of it.

'A spy who wants to disappear.'

The train shook, clattering over points. He imagined a river of darkness rushing below his feet, a bottomless black into which he longed to fall.

'Spying is a dangerous game,' replied Mulcahy, accenting his point with a circular stroke of his index finger.

'It's not a game. It's my life.'

Mulcahy pressed him with more questions, but Kant was unable to answer, distracted by the movement of the Chief of Staff's fingers, like a dumb animal following the whip of its expert trainer.

He closed his eyes and drifted into unconsciousness. 'Leave me alone,' he mumbled.

Collins patted Mulcahy on his shoulder. 'Look at him. He looks like he might die in an hour.'

'Who's he trying to disappear from?'

'From himself, perhaps?'

The voices revolved in his head, the words turning in upon themselves.

'It's impossible to tell what some of these Englishmen are really up to in Dublin,' said Collins. 'I've met Bolsheviks, anarchists, pacifists, ruthless spies and hardened criminals. They fight in the strangest of ways. They seem more interested in throwing sand in each other's eyes, than landing a punch on the enemy's face.'

'They are the madmen of our time. They've been waiting for a war like ours to come along.'

The couplings between the carriages strained as they gathered speed. Kant opened his eyes briefly and watched the green signal lights flying past the window.

'My contact in Dublin Castle says he knows him,' said Collins

'Then he is a spy, and his story of a lust murderer is a set of lies.' Mulcahy's splayed fingers hung in the air.

'I don't know. I think he's mostly truthful.'

'He's confused. Delirious.'

'He'll say anything to survive.'

'You think these missing women were murdered?'

'I might be wrong.'

'You seldom are.' Mulcahy rested his fingers against his lips.

'I can be mistaken and duped like any other man.'

'You don't sound mistaken. You must have reason to believe his story is correct.'

'There is a connection between these women, one that Mr Kant has not yet uncovered. I believe they were lured from Dublin Castle by an English spy.'

'Then at least part of his story is true.' Mulcahy leaned closer to Kant, his fingers drawing a pattern over the reporter's ashen face, as though they might draw the truth from him.

'I think Mr Kant is entirely truthful, based on the sort of fellow he is,' said Collins.

'What sort is that?'

'A directionless Englishman, who no longer wishes to live an ordinary life.'

'You make him sound dangerous.'

'That's undoubtedly true.'

'Will you have him shot?'

The train released a high-pitched whistle and the carriage shuddered as it sped into the darkness of a long tunnel. Kant felt himself plunge forwards, shooting through the carriages as if they were mirages, until he was riding at the very front of the screaming train, and then he heard nothing more.

He jerked awake with a gasp. Mulcahy had disappeared, and an absolute silence had fallen upon the carriage. The faces of Collins and his men were grey and devoid of emotion. They leaned in upon the reporter, pressing him heavily against the window. He saw that the squad member next to the door had his gun drawn and half-concealed in his lap. It took Kant several moments to realise the reason for their tension – the train had drawn to a complete stop.

Collins hunched forward and peered through the snow-covered window.

'Do you think the train's stranded in a drift?' asked one of his men.

'If it is, we'll make the guards dig us out. At gunpoint.'

Time seemed to pass slowly. The thickness of the silence and the stares of the squad made the carriage feel even more oppressive. Kant looked through the window, his brain jamming blind in the white glare of the snow. He closed his eyes, rested his head against the glass, slipped in and out of sleep.

He awoke with the uncomfortable sensation of someone staring at him. He opened his eyes a little and saw a British soldier peering into the carriage from the corridor. He stirred himself awake, rising rapidly through levels of consciousness to a heightened awareness. He breathed in sharply as a column of soldiers made their way along the corridor. He glanced outside. Another line of soldiers marched up and down the train tracks, their guns raised at the carriage windows.

Collins and his men looked at each other in silence, their faces lean and hungry-looking. For the first time that morning, they looked uncertain of what to do next. Kant, on the other hand, felt as though he had been pulled back from a dangerous borderline. If only he could communicate a message to the soldiers or the train guards, he might still be saved.

A soldier opened the door and poked his head inside. Collins immediately chuckled and wished him a cheery good morning, his face changing in an instant, his features growing big and rounded, his expression genial and relaxed, as though he were now inhabiting the body of a country businessman on a trip to the city. Kant believed he had discovered Collins' special talent. The IRA leader could change his appearance and persona at will, throwing aside personalities like ballast. By contrast, his squad seemed to go inert, like sacks of flour.

The soldier asked Collins for his identification papers. Collins flourished them from his wallet and waggled them at the soldier, still with a teasing smile playing on his lips. The soldier snapped the papers from his hand and examined them carefully. He looked at Collins, and using the butt of his rifle, lifted the fringe of hair hanging over the IRA man's forehead. Collins stared back at him, keeping the humour in his eyes. A look of recognition or contempt flashed in the soldier's eyes. He handed the papers back to Collins and left the carriage. Sharp voices sounded in the corridor, discussing something, and then came the march of heavy boots approaching.

'Hold your weapons until I give the order,' Collins warned his men, his features sharpening again. Kant had seen Mick Collins the forceful gunman sink almost out of sight, and then surface again. The train rocked slightly with the boarding of more soldiers, and the feeling of tension in the carriage intensified. An inner force was working on Collins' face, pulling his lips into an open-mouthed half-grin. He stared at the door, waiting for the signal to start firing. His henchmen grew impatient as time ticked by. One of them leaned over to open a crack in the door.

'Wait,' said Collins. They could hear soldiers' feet marching back down the corridor and then all went quiet. Someone ran by the window. Kant peered through the glass, but the only thing he could see was a low winter sun angling out of the sky, glittering upon the freshly fallen drifts.

Eventually a small man, wearing wire-rimmed glasses,

and dressed in the uniform of a train guard, entered the carriage with an embarrassed cough.

'Mr Collins,' he said, 'the passenger in the next carriage would like you and Mr Kant to join him over a bottle of whiskey.'

'I don't drink while on business,' replied Collins with a growl, and then, 'how do you know our names?'

The guard looked even more uncomfortable. 'Pardon me, Mr Collins. The passenger said his name was General Jack Stapleton, Head of Department G in Dublin Castle. He said he has a spot of business to discuss with you.'

FOURTEEN

The engine started up and the train rolled forward as the guard led Collins and Kant down the corridor. He tapped on the door of the next carriage and a growl sounded from within, which they took to be an invitation to enter.

Kant recognised the upright bearing of the man seated at the table, his vigorous features and his raised chin; however, his gaze had changed. General Stapleton's eyes were wasted-looking and watery as he looked up from his bottle of whiskey.

'Forgive me, Mr Collins, for interrupting your journey,' said the general. He seemed anxious to show the IRA leader respect. 'I thought we might have a glass of whiskey or two and work out how to save Ireland from this terrible war. I assume you like to discuss military strategy?'

If the invitation surprised Collins, he did not show it. He behaved as if this was what sworn enemies did from time to time.

'I always like to discuss strategy. Day and night.' Collins returned the general's stare with a quizzical glare.

'Fine, then let us drink together.' The general's voice grew warm-spirited, and his eyes glittered. He seemed to be taking a special relish in the IRA leader's company.

'I don't like drinking whiskey, though,' said Collins, untruthfully.

'Come on Mr Collins, drink,' said the general. 'A man of war should drink like a fish.'

'If a man of war drinks like a fish then he has packed in serious soldiery.'

'I know why you are reluctant to drink; you think that I am here with this bottle of whiskey to lure you into a trap.'

'No,' said Collins, hesitating. 'I think it highly unlikely that the British army has started using generals as bait.' He sat down at the table, and Stapleton smiled.

'You're quite correct. We let the lower ranks do our dirty work.' The general glanced at Kant who had shuffled alongside Collins and now leaned back against the seat like a flagging boxer resting between rounds. The general poured the three of them a glass of whiskey. Collins inspected the amber liquid for a moment and then knocked it back. A little gas stove had been placed close to the general, and the air gradually grew warm and heavy.

'War is strange is it not?' said the general. 'How it gives men like you and I the illusion that we are irreconcilable strangers, but in reality it brings us closer together in all sorts of interesting ways.'

'How has it done that?'

'Through this file of missing women that our *Daily Mirror* reporter has compiled.'

'What do you know about these crimes?' asked Collins.

'Enough to suspect that someone in Dublin Castle is behind them.'

'These are no ordinary acts of war. The girls were savagely murdered.'

'I agree completely. In the circumstances, I think it's vital that we talk about preventing further victims, in particular, Lily Merrin.'

'Who do you mean by we?'

'You and I. And Mr Kant, of course.'

'I don't want to do any talking about Lily Merrin.'

'I think I speak for all of us when I say her safety is paramount.'

The train was back at full speed, making a racket, the carriage rocking as it raced past snow-draped backstreets. Kant's sense of being a stranger crossing unfamiliar territory deepened. He wondered if Stapleton's invitation had increased the threat of danger or lessened it.

'Tell me, why did you have the train stopped?' asked Collins.

'I could tell you that I was meant to board it first thing this morning. That there was a mix up in my diary and I was delayed. That my men stopped it so I could board mid-transit, and that by chance, I picked the carriage next to yours. That's one version of the truth. The other is that my men have been following your every move since yesterday evening.'

Collins emptied his glass and rose. 'I think Mr Kant and I shall leave now,' he said, heaving the reporter to his feet.

The general eyed Kant with a measure of concern. 'What do you plan to do with our *Daily Mirror* reporter?' he asked.

'Mr Kant is anxious to help me with some enquiries I am making.' He pushed the reporter to the door and glanced back at Stapleton. 'I understand your worry for your missing typist. For a man in your position it must seem uniquely unfair, in fact a torment to have a member of staff disappear like that. But so many people go missing at a time of war. People a great deal more innocent than our Mr Kant. And each situation has its own brand of unfairness, but I am unable to assist you any further.' He saluted and made to leave the compartment.

'Wait,' said the general. 'A lunatic spy is on the loose, targeting Irish women, and you have no wish to stop him in his tracks?'

'With all the murder and mayhem perpetrated by your soldiers I hadn't noticed,' said Collins, but he hesitated. His eyes glinted as he worked out the strategic advantages of the general's difficulty.

'I wouldn't want to be the republican leader who passed by on the chance of apprehending this maniac,' said the general. 'Think of the harm he will do if he continues unchecked.'

'I agree that this murderer should be stopped.'

'What do you suggest we do?' asked Stapleton.

'Suggest?' replied Collins, a note of anger in his voice. 'I suggest that we each take responsibility and discipline our own men. And if anyone steps out of line they should be court-martialled.'

'How well do you know your recruits?'

'As well as a father knows his sons.'

'Then you should know that in every army there are monsters lurking in the shadows. Men who have no limits when it comes to evil. At times, I wish I could see in the souls of my men. I'd like a glimpse of what's there, but to be honest, I don't know if I'd care to peer too deeply.'

'Is it any wonder such crimes are being committed against Irish women when you consider the filth that you are sending over?'

'Filth?' said the general quietly.

'I'm not talking about your soldiers, although you must admit there are more rogues than saints among their ranks.

I'm talking about the droves of spies that are infiltrating the city. Dublin is like a wound crawling with maggots. The boarding houses are full of cut-throats, touts, bullies, crooks, swindlers and rapists. All of them greedy for the enormous reward offered for my capture. All of them ably supported by your intelligence services.'

The general smiled. 'Maggots are our friends. They might tickle and look unpleasant but they have a special talent at cleaning wounds. One just needs to turn a blind eye and let them burrow into the deepest corners.'

'Your blind eye has allowed this murderer free rein.'

'Which is why I am asking you to assist Mr Kant in hunting him down.'

Collins' eyes were cold and calculating. 'What can you offer me in exchange?'

'Security and something more important. A political solution to this conflict.'

Collins chuckled quietly. 'Not much has amused me lately, but your offer has. What sort of security can an English general offer me on my own soil?'

'The bounty on your head has been raised to £10,000. Dublin Castle will keep raising it until you are caught.'

'Right now, I can watch my own back, and half of Dublin Castle's, for that matter.'

The train roared into a tunnel, ghostly flecks of grey ash clinging to the windows. When it emerged into daylight, the two men were leaning closer together. Their voices grew lower, half drowned by the pounding and clatter of the train.

'That is the problem with leaders like you and I,' said the general, his voice almost vanishing under the sound of the glancing wheels. 'We are too caught up in the fray. Too entangled in this bloody conflict to realise that it is war itself we should be fighting and not each other.'

'Your argument has a pragmatic ring to it.' Collins' voice had also developed a strangely intimate tone.

'That is because I'm arguing with a pragmatist.'

'So what weapons should we be taking into battle?'

'The art of compromise. Political negotiation. Lloyd George does not want to risk another terrible war, especially when so much international opinion is on the side of small nations like Ireland. Privately, he has instructed his generals to extract a constitutional settlement with the Republican Army.'

Collins gave a snort of frustration.

'Mr Collins, you are a realist, a practical man surrounded by bloodthirsty rebels with clumsy aspirations. Look out the window. This is not a country ready for a violent revolution.'

Collins knocked back his whiskey and thought for a while. He smiled. 'Strange how one can be more daring in planning military strategy with a bottle of whiskey and one's enemy for company.'

The general moistened his lips with his glass. 'Some of the best decisions are made in the most unusual circumstances.' He watched Collins closely. 'I am under few illusions in this war. The only two people who can stop it are the Prime Minister and you. The future of Ireland will depend on the compromises you will reach one day. For this reason, I am speaking quite openly with you, and I hope the position is mutual.'

Collins said nothing, his thick fringe hanging loosely over his forehead. The train clattered over points and his thickset torso jostled against Kant, as if he were drunk, or sleeping.

'Let us raise a toast,' said the general, eyeing Collins.

'In whose name?'

'In the name of Ireland. North and South.'

'What did you say?'

'Two Irelands, not one. Two countries, full of free Irishmen, but not united. I'm sure, given time and careful thought, you will agree there is no other possible option for the land you hold dear.'

The general downed his drink and poured another.

Collins was about to protest, but a strange look fell over the general's face. The skin was drawn tight about his face, and not a muscle moved. Unexpectedly, tears began to well in his eyes.

'There is something I have to tell you,' said the general in a firm voice, in spite of the wetness in his eyes. 'In every battle, military men like you and I hope for swift progress, to advance with only a handful of casualties. None of us expect or hope for carnage.' The general emptied his glass and replenished it. 'But I have ordered lines of boys, barely 18 or 19, many of them Irish, into a hurricane of German gunfire. I'm talking about the Somme and Verdun. I'd seen a lot of violence in my life, and I'd grown hardened to mutilation, but in the spring of 1918 I watched young men die in quantities I had not dreamed possible. I prayed to God to let it all stop, that no more soldiers should die in vast waves like that. But the regiments kept marching in their thousands to the front-line and I kept sending our boys over. Half of England, and Ireland, too.'

'You should have ordered them to stop.'

'You can order soldiers to die but you can't order them to stay alive by running from a Lewis gun. No military leader has ever issued an order like that.'

'What makes you think my war of independence will end in carnage, too? The republican army has more than 10,000 men at its disposal. Our will to win is formidable. We are organised in a mighty wave of resistance. I have no doubt that our military success will deliver an independent Irish nation within months.'

'These days a successful soldier must also be a politician.'

'What do you mean?'

'Ulster is your intractable problem. The major obstacle to a united Ireland. Loyalty to the King throbs in the lifeblood of its Protestant people. If I was leader I would rather surrender Ulster to the British and go against the concerns of diehard republicans than risk a long and bloody war.'

'Any political solution that does not include complete Irish independence shall be rejected by Sinn Fein's ruling council.'

'What about the many ordinary Irishmen who believe that this bloody war cannot be settled except by political means?'

'What are you talking about? Compromise? Capitulation to the Crown?'

'I haven't mentioned either. Only negotiation.'

A gloomy look fell over Collins' face. 'What you are suggesting is tantamount to treachery.'

'What do you mean by treachery?'

'Treachery in betraying the cause of Irish freedom.'

'No, treachery in this particular situation is more terrible than that. Treachery is indifference to the suffering of Irish men and women. That is the truest form of betrayal.'

The train rattled on, and for a long time neither man spoke. The general and Collins kept drinking, and the more they knocked away, the more Kant could feel Collins' body leaning into his. The proximity of the IRA leader and the watchful stare of the general gave him an odd feeling of being included and accepted, that he was indispensable to this meeting of military leaders. He sat without moving, listening to the steady breathing of Collins' chest, the pauses in between. The rasp in his own chest quietened and he felt a sense of well-being flood his veins that may also have had a lot to do with the general's whiskey.

The general interrupted the silence. 'To assist the British government in any negotiations with Sinn Fein, I need a direct link to you. A path of communication that will remain hidden to the prying eyes of Dublin Castle, and the rest of Sinn Fein.' The general slowly swung his attention to Kant. 'I propose an additional role for our *Daily Mirror* reporter while he is searching for Lily Merrin. We should use him as our liaison channel, in advance of peace negotiations. Our go-between to communicate important messages.'

Kant shifted in his seat, suddenly feeling very much out of his depth. He waited for more, but both the general and Collins remained silent.

'You have been very quiet, Mr Kant,' said the general. 'What is your opinion on this matter?'

'Don't be coy,' added Collins. 'You opened this can of worms. In my book that means you should close it.'

'Just to be clear, general, who do I take my orders from? You or Mr Collins.'

'You should follow Mr Collins' advice to the letter. Just get this business settled and find Lily Merrin. I don't want a complicated, drawn-out investigation. I want it closed as quickly and effectively as possible.'

'Do you mean closed or resolved?' asked Kant.

'Mr Collins will tell you precisely what I mean.'

The general stared at Collins waiting for his response.

'Two weeks, Mr Kant.' Collins squeezed Kant affectionately on the shoulder. 'I will lend you and the general two weeks to find Lily Merrin. I will ensure your safety and assist your search. After that time, you must be gone. Any extra expenditure will cost you your life.'

Kant thought of the reports he had compiled, feeling as though he had fallen into a trap of his own devising. 'I'm honoured to be given this assignment,' he said. However, his tone expressed much less than wholehearted enthusiasm for the task that lay ahead.

When they left the carriage, Collins' face took on its hungry edge again. He slapped Kant forcefully on the back.

'You're a fully-fledged spy now, Mr Kant. Your wish has finally been granted.'

Kant could feel the train shaking, the tracks rumbling below. Collins broke into laughter, the sound welling up like a black pool about to engulf him. The IRA leader leaned towards him, his eyes glittering with amusement.

'Remember this, Mr Kant, you do not become a spy to find your identity, but to lose it.' He spoke in an easy drawl. The train began to slow to a stop, lurching them closer together. 'You must make yourself a void, my dear reporter, one that lurks in other people's secrets. You must become silence. And don't forget, silence is very hard to live with, especially silence in the middle of a teeming city like Dublin.' The stilling of the wheels made his voice suddenly very loud and clear. 'Real silence is death, and this is every man's worst fear. It will be very hard for you as a spy with so many of your bloodthirsty countrymen around you. You must become more silent than the silent spies in the deepest shadows. You must wait until you can hear silence itself speak.'

The train doors opened and Collins stepped out into the white gusting light. He was still smiling when he disappeared from view, letting the crowd of disembarking passengers carry his broad-shouldered frame into their midst, as though the mass of bodies was his movement, his flock, his following.

It was night by the time Kant returned to his ransacked bedroom. From the darkness of the landing, he heard the creak of a briefcase handle. A bony hand dangling out of a worn coat squeezed the faded leather tightly. From the shadows rose the thin figure of Brugha, like a dry husk sucked up by a breeze.

'What are you doing here?' asked Kant.

'I've been following you. Watching you on the streets, and in the pubs. I've been waiting to see what sort of knave you are.'

'And what have you found?'

'You are careful and watchful, and have a talent for embroiling yourself in conspiracy. Ordinarily, people whose lives are under threat, they try to run away, but not you.'

'I have a job to do. Working as a reporter takes me into dark corners.'

'They say you are also a British spy, which makes you somewhat unreliable, but in the circumstances you suit me fine. I think I can trust you with my secret. I've read your little report in the *Daily Mirror* about the missing women. I can furnish you with a much more interesting story that might be your paper's scoop of the year.'

'Which is what?'

'Collins the bastard has been trying to sideline me because

I suspect he has been gambling away the IRA finances. But some day soon his turn will come. A double-crosser like that will not survive forever.' His bitterness seemed concentrated in his thin red lips.

'How do you plan to stop him?'

'With the correct pieces of information, a single bureaucrat can bring down an entire army.' His knuckles tightened their hold on the briefcase. He kept it close to his body, as though it were a child that needed singing to and rocked. What would it take to make him surrender its contents, wondered Kant.

'Mick is obsessed with paper. Everything is filed and recorded, every meeting, every contact. He knows that whoever keeps the record, has the power, the advantage. It's not a war he's running, it's an army of typewriters battering away in cramped offices all over the city, churning out a 10,000 word fiction, the deepest lie ever told. Mick Collins. Ireland's greatest rebel.' Brugha gave a dispirited smile. 'Mick the super spy confounding British intelligence, Mick the gun-runner ordering Tommy guns from the production line, Mick the financial wizard bankrolling the rebellion from 1,000 secret accounts, Mick the commander-in-chief and minister of everything, an enormous discrepancy that grows bigger by the day.'

He paused, stared at Kant, and blinked back a look of gloating delight.

'To keep a fiction like that going requires a lot of editing,' he continued. 'Mick has been quietly deleting any evidence that might tarnish his reputation. However, my little briefcase has a special appetite for his burnt pieces of paper, all the discarded scraps of writing, the half-destroyed notes. It can home in on them from miles away.' Brugha's hands locked tight on the briefcase's handle. His eyes widened with excitement. 'They are my secret cargo, my antidote to Mick's meticulous notebooks, a counterforce to his propaganda and politics. They carry a truth someone wants to extinguish, which is why I am keen to gather them up.'

Kant felt chilled to the bone and tired from the day's exertions. His breath rattled in his chest. All he wanted to do was drop into his bed and sleep.

'To tell you the truth, I don't know what to think of Collins. I don't know what is going on with him and the republican army, nor do I know what Dublin Castle are up to. How do you think I can help you?'

Was it pity he saw in Brugha's eyes or just tiredness?

'I want you to look out for pieces of paper with Mick's signature. Hold onto them for me before he destroys them. They will help us uncover the truth.'

He tipped his hat at Kant and fled down the stairs into the night, clutching the briefcase close to his chest. It was not so much a matter of him being able to let go of the briefcase, realised Kant. In the half-light, it looked like a swollen parasite that would not release its grip on him, searching for a way into his thin body.

FIFTEEN

It was the hour of dawn and Kant stood across the empty square from Dublin Castle, the nerve centre of British intelligence in Ireland, its inviolable fortress of secrets. The square echoed with the sound of women banging on the castle gates and shouting. They were the grieving relatives of the murdered women, and had been there all night, chanting prayers, singing hymns and waving placards, with a hungry, agitated edge to their grief, like that of mothers who had hung around too long at the side of a battlefield.

Kant had spent the last three days in bed, recovering from the fever he had caught on his early morning train journey with Collins. He knew that he had been lucky. The IRA men had intended he catch something much more permanent. For short periods during the day, he was able to rise and work at his typewriter, writing pieces for the press in London, pouring out what he considered twaddle, details of British reprisals for IRA attacks that came straight from Dublin Castle, sanitised of any of the violent excesses of British soldiers. The reports were just enough to satisfy his bosses in London and help him keep his job.

In the cold air and dazzle of the early morning sun, he found it uncomfortable standing still, his legs were tired and his eyes blinked in the golden light. All he could see were the needle-like shadows of the protesting women, jabbing against the sun-burnished bars.

When the gates opened to let in the civilian staff, he struck off gingerly, using his cane for support, pushing his way through the shawled women. They swelled around him with their dark, menacing faces, and looked ready to pounce on him until a Scottish sentry intervened, shouting and waving his rifle in the air.

'Bloody Catholic mothers,' said the Scot to the reporter as the throng piled against the gates. 'They dare to bless themselves in public and pray for their rebel daughters. Right in front of our noses, too.' He looked aghast.

As if on signal, the women began a loud recitation of the rosary, a flurry of Hail Marys erupting into the air.

The sentry growled again. 'Praying all over the place. They didn't warn me they were sending me to a Papist zoo.'

On the other side of the gates, Kant found even less tranquillity. The stomping of marching boots, and the rattling of spurs and weapons reigned supreme. A regiment paraded in full field dress, practising their drills in rows of four. Kant waited as the soldiers swung past, followed by a horseman riding the largest grey mare he had ever seen. The horse, picking its way through the soldiers, seemed to take fright at something and reared backwards. The rider pressed in his heels and shook the reins, but the animal became more agitated, swinging its large head back and forth, frothing at the bit, its eyes brimming with fear. The column of marching men broke rank and parted like a frightened herd, but the rider kept holding the horse back. At one point, he turned in Kant's direction, revealing a proud, chiselled face that looked simultaneously bored and amused. The rider waved at Kant in recognition. It was Corporal Isham. With a lazy looking shake of the reins, he spun the horse round, and drove it towards the castle stables.

Kant walked through a stone archway and into the main hall of the British war office. Exalted ceilings rose above a long room full of earnest young men pounding the marble floors, gabbling to each other, exchanging files from boxes and briefcases. From a room at the end of a corridor came the jabbing sounds of about a dozen intent typists. Kant queued at the main desk from where he hoped to gain access to the intelligence archives.

In front of him, an elderly woman with discoloured grey hair spoke in long hysterical sobs, while waving a handful of crumpled papers at the harassed looking clerk at the desk.

She turned and wailed at the rest of the queue. 'God save me, they've forgotten my dead husband already.'

From what Kant could make out, her husband had been an employee at the castle, leaving her entitled to a monthly pension. However, the previous payment had been reduced to a fraction of the usual sum, without any explanation whatsoever. The clerk had examined the papers and kept claiming Dublin Castle had not issued the pension in the first place.

'This has nothing to do with us,' he insisted, shrugging his shoulders. 'You've come to the wrong place. You must go to the banks that issued the payments. There are several ones mentioned in your letters.'

'I've been to every bank in Dublin, and they've all turned

me away. The last manager told me to take the file here.'

The clerk was unwilling to help her any further, and turned to the next person in the line, but the woman waved the papers in his face and pleaded with him. Eventually he gave way to her clamouring insistence and fetched a colleague from a side-room. For a few minutes, the woman appeared gratified and relaxed her protestations.

'What imbecile has sent you to Dublin Castle?' The second clerk erupted into a vile temper after he had studied the file. 'There is nothing we can do for you.' He tried to take her roughly by the arm and lead her out of the building but she burst into tears and sank to her knees, shaking the papers at anyone who cared to look. Eventually, the exasperated clerk found a chair for her, and went off in search of his superior.

The manager gazed at her with unblinking eyes. 'Why have you come here?' he asked.

'Because you are the authorities.'

'But we don't pay your husband's pension,' he explained. 'Consequently, we are powerless to correct this mistake.'

'If you do nothing I shall make a complaint.'

It seemed pointless. The old woman was impenetrable to logic and indifferent to their scorn and frustration. The manager threw his hands in the air and sighed. 'Sit down and one of the secretaries will bring you a cup of tea.'

She hefted her bag of papers to one side, and eventually Kant reached the front of the queue. He presented his identification to the manager, who dug out a typed letter from a drawer.

'Martin Kant. British Intelligence, Section C. Temporary transfer regarding...'

The manager hesitated and looked perplexed. 'Strange.

They haven't filled in the rest of the sheet.'

With a doubtful look, he stamped Kant's identity card.

'The information in the intelligence archive is operational. Everything in it is watched very closely.'

The gas lit cellars stocking the archive were long and winding like a labyrinth and lined with six-foot-high metal shelving. Kant's footsteps echoed as though someone else were walking to meet him from a far off corridor. He found a pale clerk, who looked as though he had not left the underworld of the castle in a decade. He asked for the intelligence files on Collins. The clerk disappeared and returned with a series of large volumes.

'Mr Collins has become so notorious, we hold more information on him than the Vatican keeps of the devil,' he said.

Kant opened the most recent volume. The only thing of note in the reports was the fact that they were riddled with contradictions and discrepancies. The IRA leader's eyes were blue in a description from November 1918. By January, they were dark brown. In June, they were green and by September, they were blue again. Alternate reports described him as a young man of fair complexion, clean-shaven, wearing a slight moustache, cold, harsh, cruel-faced, short in stature, tall and wiry, broad and heavy in build, greatly out of condition, youthful, looking about forty, fat but virile, dressed like a clerk, a publican, a stockbroker, or something in the city. One agent warned, 'he can present a perfectly blank appearance and cannot be picked out of a crowd unless you know him'. His hair was alternatively described as a soft brown mop, or as a jet-black mass.

Kant handed the clerk the reference code for the file Merrin had given him on the day she disappeared, and asked for directions to where it had been shelved. He hoped the neighbouring files might shed light on its mysterious list of numbers and dates.

The clerk frowned and looked disconcerted.

'Where did you get the code?'

'From a contact.'

'Did the contact have the actual file?'

'No.'

'I was hoping that perhaps it might have been rescued...' He left the sentence hanging in the air, as if unsure of how to finish it.

'What do you mean rescued?'

The clerk gave him directions to where the file had been stored. 'You'll find out what I mean when we get there.'

He escorted the reporter down a damp corridor and left him at an alcove filled with a different, earthier odour to the rest of the archives. The gas lamp above the recess threw enough light to reveal what at first Kant thought were the signs of neglect and decay, but then realised were the remnants of a fire, the metal filing cabinets scorched black, a fine layer of ashes coating the shelves. The section containing the other files relating to Merrin's stolen dossier appeared to have been at the centre of the blaze. He ran his hands along the ashes and was reminded of the fire in Merrin's boarding house bedroom.

The sound of approaching footsteps interrupted him from his reverie.

Spectral in the gaslight, a figure appeared in the corridor. 'Hello, Kant.' It was Isham. 'Fancy finding you grubbing about here. I thought you fellows preferred to be out at large and not stuck in a crypt like this.'

'Just following orders.'

'Whose?' Isham's eyes were blank.

'General Stapleton's.'

Again an empty gaze.

'I have to say, you'll not make much progress in here.' Isham flicked through a row of files in the opposite alcove to hide his irritation. 'You know this is not really an intelligence archive in the strictest sense of the word. You'll not find names or dates or identifying traits that will lead you to the enemy. What you see here is nothing more than the popular Irish wish of getting one up on one's neighbours.' He turned deeper into the murky shadows between the shelves. It was so gloomy Kant could barely see him at all. 'If you listen closely, you can hear the endless whispering, the malicious gossip, the petty complaints in a hundred different bog and mountain accents, the layers of parish rivalries that go back generations. It is unfortunate, but our intelligence system has allowed all this bitterness to rise to the surface.'

'You're depressing me.'

'Take it as advice from one professional to another. You're wasting your time burrowing away in a place like this. The enemy is out there.'

'Where?'

'Everywhere. Strolling through the streets, drinking in the pubs, betting on the races, praying in the churches…'

'Thank you, corporal. I've been warned. By the way, what happened to the files in this section?'

'Oh those, they were burned to cinders.'

'Why?'

'Why do fires usually start? Because of stupidity, carelessness. One of the clerks was dim-witted enough to leave a candle burning. By the time the idiot raised the alarm, the whole alcove was ablaze. General Stapleton should really close the entire place down to everyone but the intelligence chiefs. The whole place could go up like tinder.'

He joined Kant in the alcove, sniffing at the stench of damp ashes.

'Between you and me, Kant, the general is driving us all mad. He wants to turn our spies into peace envoys. Every day he rants about pulling back and not provoking Collins.'

'The general is very dedicated to his goals of a political settlement.'

Isham eyed the reporter closely. 'I hear a rumour he's appointed you as an intermediary with Sinn Fein.'

'I'm sure I'm not the first spy from Dublin Castle asked to make secret contact with the IRA.' He watched Isham for a reaction, but there was none.

'My dear Mr Kant,' said the corporal in a tone that was somewhere between polite distaste and ironic respect, 'have you ever stopped to consider what the general has really planned for you? Why he dropped you in this difficult role at such short notice?'

'I don't have an answer to that. I'm not sure what exactly he wants me to do, or why he even asked me in the first place.'

'Let me give you a hint. Stapleton is a career general, and a cunning one at that. He wants to seal his reputation with one final historic victory before he retires. Right now, he's filing a report outlining how he has brought Collins to the brink of a political compromise. Keep digging around the disappearance of Merrin and you risk alienating Collins and messing up Stapleton's plans for a grand success. Think about it carefully.'

'What if there is a madman out there murdering women for the thrill of it? What if he's one of ours, working under the protection of Dublin Castle?'

The clock tower in the castle began to chime the hour. It had a grave bass note. Afterwards there was an uncomfortable silence during which Isham kept glaring at the reporter.

'Let me make one thing clear,' said Isham at last, as if he'd been considering if that one thing was worth explaining to the reporter. His voice was his own now, no longer convivial, but cold and arrogant. 'No one in Dublin Castle is interested in how these women were murdered. Their deaths are regarded as stray events, part of the arbitrary nature of things during war. But we are interested in the bigger picture. And it is important that you should be discreet in your investigations.' The shadows of his face grew deeper. 'Think about this, if Collins becomes hell bent on war and rejects the general's peace overtures, Stapleton will be able to blame you and your meddling. He might even accuse you of being an agent provocateur and have you arrested. Who knows? I might even shop you in myself.' He flashed a sardonic grin.

Kant shrugged. 'Right now I'm more interested in finding out what happened to Lily Merrin. And so should you and the rest of Dublin Castle.'

'Before you get carried away with your little investigation, let me tell you something of what I've learned about Collins. He's a black-hearted, thorough-going spawn of the bog women-hater.' Isham's eyes did not blink once as he stared at the reporter. 'But he's also a clever bastard. He has recruited a circle of devoted IRA women, who regard him as their hero, their great liberator, because he sets them tasks straight from the pages of a fantasy spy novel. He has given them faith in their powers as individuals, and in return, they show him undying loyalty. If anyone is behind the disappearance of Merrin it is Collins. He has made these female recruits his unquestioning slaves. He has turned secretaries into spies, typists into terrorists, nuns into assassins, expectant mothers into gun smugglers. And whenever they have served their useful purpose, they become expendable.'

'Sounds like you know him quite well.'

'I've been busy with my sources. Much better than sniffing in the dirt of this place.'

'What can you tell me about Collins and the IRA's finances?' Now it was Kant's turn to watch Isham closely.

Isham shrugged. 'He's been fiddling around with substantial amounts of money. What makes you so interested in his spending habits?'

'Just following a line of enquiry, that's all.'

'Who suggested the enquiry?'

'A member of Sinn Fein's ruling council. A man called Cathal Brugha.'

Isham relaxed a little, as though the conversation had been pulled back from a dangerous brink. He stared at Kant, expecting further detail, but at that moment, Kant leaned against the shelves, and broke into a coughing fit. His chest sounded more alarming with its rattling echoing back from the dank cellar walls.

'It's none of my business,' said Isham, 'but I don't think Dublin is doing you any good. It's too full of smoke and too near the sea. Damp all year round. Why don't you go back to England, or Scotland even? Get a post up in the hills, away from these clouds of charcoal and ash.'

'Dublin isn't good for any of us. But I have a mission here. A sense of direction and purpose that gives me satisfaction.'

'Not for much longer, I'm afraid. You'll soon see that you're here like the rest of us. By accident. The only sense of direction we have is the one carrying us blindly towards death.'

Neither spoke for a while.

'It'll be Christmas, soon,' said Isham, turning to leave. 'Make sure you don't work yourself into an early grave.'

When Kant returned to the front hall of the war office, he saw that the old woman was still there. By now, she had set off a black panic of vexation among the clerks and their manager. The more annoyed they became, the more emboldened were her pleas.

The manager was trying to control the exasperation in his voice. 'I keep telling you, the pension is paid through separate bank accounts, not Dublin Castle,' he explained.

'Why would the banks pay me a pension when my husband never worked for them? He worked here. At Dublin Castle. It's you who have made the mistake, not me.'

The manager threw his arms in the air as if the old woman's insistence was a criminal provocation. He marched away, his face plunged into desperation, leaving the old woman on her own, muttering to herself. Kant went over to her and offered his assistance. She stepped forward, as if about to faint, and he grabbed her. He ignored what she was gabbling about and concentrated on reading the bundle of papers that the clerks had scorned. He saw a death certificate, letters from the British War Office, and details of a pension paid through a company registered on Leeson Street.

There were dozens of signatures in the documents, which alerted Kant's curiosity. They suggested a complex financial machinery. Several times, he spotted the address of the Dublin Life Assurance Company, and in a jumble of signatures, he made out in blotched, barely legible handwriting, the name of a man that burned him with the white-hot iron of a dangerous secret. The name was Michael Collins, and next to it was the signature of Moya Llewelyn Davies, the aristocratic owner of Furry Park, and a well-known republican sympathiser. He was at pains not to show his surprise. The clerks and their manager had obviously not bothered to scrutinise the finer details of the pension. Now that he had spotted the names, they were unignorable, hovering above the flat figures and account details, perfect and complete-looking in spite of their hurried scrawl. He tracked them through the documents. The payments into the woman's bank had been made from a number of ordinary deposit accounts from obscure banks, sometimes in the name of the Dublin Life Assurance Company, and sometimes in others.

'Who asked you to fill in the pension application form?' he asked her.

'A man came to the door one night after my husband died.'

'Which department was he from?'

'He didn't say.' She gripped his arm. A coldness passed through her fingers. She had seen the look of uneasiness on his face.

'Is there any reason why the Republican Army might be paying your husband's pension?'

A look of fear fluttered across her gaunt features. She mouthed a prayer in silence. 'Sweet Jesus, why would those murdering bastards be paying a pension for my poor Oliver?'

SIXTEEN

With his wheezing cough and English accent, Kant felt ill-suited to the company as he made his way through the packed bar in Vaughn's Hotel. Collins had marched into his bedroom that evening, and ordered him to get dressed. Without saying a further word, he had walked out, leaving the door open. It took a moment for the reporter to realise the IRA leader was inviting him on an expedition. He had followed Collins' broad shoulders onto the street and through a labyrinth of back alleyways, eventually descending a dank set of steps, into the cellars and then up another flight and through the front door of the offices next to the hotel.

He passed a gruesome gallery of drunken IRA types, who looked as though they had gathered for a night's entertainment and debauchery. He felt the crowd swarm around him, closing in tightly, people shouting and joyfully yelling, laughing heartily and embracing each other, while above their heads, borne aloft by waiters' hard-working hands, floated frothy pints of stout.

Collins guided Kant by placing a hand on his shoulder and squeezing it tightly. He was wearing a soft grey business suit, and twirled a hat with an elegantly dented crown in his hand. He reminded Kant of a man who had just come from a wedding or a day at the races.

The IRA leader's eyes were eager and hard.

'I've an important message for your general. I want you to tell him that the old battles between Ireland and England are no more.'

'What do you mean?'

'I'm talking about battles like the Boyne or Aughrim, the orderly advance of regimented troops, the bugle-call for the charge. These days, Irish patriots hide in the shadows. Improvisation and chaos are our military strategies.' He pulled out two bar stools. 'The general wants me to steer the IRA towards peace and compromise, but he might as well ask a man to seize a racing engine wheel with his bare hands. Sit here a while and you'll soon understand what I'm talking about.'

Collins left behind his jacket and hat, and joined a stag party that had turned rowdy in a corner of the bar. He instantly assumed the role of master of revels. The men stood closely together, ringing round Collins' broad-backed form, surrounding him with alcohol-filled bravado, as he scribbled plots and diagrams on scraps of paper, and then crumpled them into little balls and flung them into the turf fire.

A group of musicians struck up a reel, and Collins began to dance through the crowd. With the men he jumped about, ducking and jabbing, feinting and bobbing. He half-wrestled one young man to the floor and roared with laughter, while with the women, he grabbed their waists playfully and twirled them in time with the music.

Kant trailed Collins as he moved randomly through the bar, surrounded by his bodyguards and a host of admirers and hangers-on. The IRA leader began questioning a police officer sympathetic to the republican cause, and at the same time, a reporter from the US newspaper, the *World's Pictorial News*, attempted to interview him for an upcoming article. In the lobby, another crowd was waiting for him, messengers with loan funds, intelligence officers with reports, officers from the country seeking arms or ammunition. Kant listened with his reporter's ear, as Collins went through them one by one, flinging out plans and proposals that made the bravest of his men shudder with dread at their impromptu recklessness. He had a mystifying gift for putting strangers at their ease and then, with a few words whispered in their ears, making their faces turn white with dread.

Collins disentangled himself from the crowd and raised his eyebrows at Kant.

'What do you see now?' His face was shining with sweat, receptive suddenly.

'Do you understand what you didn't understand before?'

He grinned at Kant as though the answer was crystal clear. When the truth finally dawned on Kant, he gave a short laugh and then he was off again, with a toss of his heavy fringe, and a flash of something like mirth in his eyes, as he plunged into the crowd of plotting IRA men. Kant realised that Collins had shown him the secret heart of his war, and revealed the innermost workings of his organisation, the key to the IRA's success – that there was no organisation at all, that a central republican command did not exist in the truest sense of the word, that targets were chosen by Collins and his men at a drunken flip of the coin, plots hatched out of jest and bravado, bombing raids conducted on a whim. All his notebooks, his countless meetings in every quadrant of the city, were just tricks to preserve the illusion that he was a mastermind at work.

Barging from one dangerous conversation to another was Collins' natural model for social contact, but Kant could see that this shambling association of spies, assassins and bodyguards was a fragile raft, perpetually on the tip of a whirlpool. With all his plots, counterplots, betrayals and secret alliances, one moment of inattention could plunge Collins' war into disorder and violence.

Kant took advantage of a pause in Collins' hectic socialising and handed him the letter from the widow.

'I rescued this from Dublin Castle', he said.

Collins read it, his eyes lighting up with recognition.

'This is the price of terminating a contract. Her husband was one of our informers in Dublin Castle, murdered by an English spy. When he died, I couldn't let his wife and his children starve. It's all part of the business of running a war.'

'Is that how you look after the relatives of all your informers, all your operatives in Dublin Castle?'

'It's only right that the IRA should look after its own.'

'What about Lily Merrin and her son?'

'Let's say her contract is a little more complicated. One that's very difficult to negotiate a termination.' Collins handed him back the letter.

'Why do I get the strange feeling I'm the only who wishes to find her?'

'What makes you say that?'

'Both you and Dublin Castle appear more interested in distracting me from my search.'

Collins grinned, turning his face into a round, inscrutable mask.

'Just tell me the truth; do you know if she is alive or dead?'

'Alive.'

'Do you want me to find her?'

'No,' he admitted. 'Lily was one of our best intelligence agents. She supplied information about upcoming raids,

Sinn Fein members on the wanted list, and most importantly of all the names of paid informers. She was smarter than all the others put together.'

'She worked for you because you kidnapped her son and used a mother's love to blackmail her. She was not spying out of personal choice.'

Collins gave a simple shrug of his shoulders. 'I like to think that we rescued her from her venal job at Dublin Castle. A place like that can be worse than prison, a counterforce to all that is good and noble in life. Her story goes deeper than anything I can tell you right now. Lily Merrin was destined to disappear right from the start, long before my men took her boy. It's a complicated story and perhaps it's best not to ask too many questions. Understand?'

'How more complicated can kidnapping and blackmail be?'

'Perhaps you'll find out the answer to that question when you work out why she went missing in the first place. I suggest you take your search back to Dublin Castle, rather than meddling in the financial matters of the Republican Army.'

'You've got my every move worked out.'

'This is a game of chess we're playing, Mr Kant.'

He was aware of Collins manipulating him, but the feeling did not cause him any anxiety or anger. After all, Collins was a magician, an escape artist. It was almost a form of entertainment.

Kant would have left at that moment but for the entrance of a man dressed in a threadbare coat and carrying a bulging briefcase. With the collar of his coat turned up against his hollow cheeks, the new arrival surveyed the crowd, his eyes adding and subtracting, multiplying and dividing, seizing upon every detail in the packed bar that might be of use for his secret collection. He caught sight of Collins at the bar, and his eyes lit up as though he had located a surprise windfall.

'Dear Jesus,' said Collins, scowling, 'What's Brugha doing here? Lugging round that bloody briefcase as though it were a suckling pig. Every time I see it, it's gained a few pounds. Look at him, its wearing him into tatters.'

Brugha's briefcase had indeed gained weight, swinging against his thin body, looking as though it was about to break open and spill its hoard of paper scraps. A tall, severe looking man joined Brugha, and they began talking. Brugha's head and shoulders were bent forward, as though bowed down by the weight of his briefcase.

'Christ, he's brought Mulcahy with him', said Collins.

Mulcahy appeared a little sad, his well-dressed frame hulking over Brugha's. When he caught sight of Collins, he waved and pointed to a door at the back of the bar.

Collins put on his jacket and hat, and dived through the crowd after them.

A hand patted Kant's arm, almost consolingly, and he turned to see the wire-rimmed glasses of O'Shea, the manager of the life assurance company. A frown criss-crossed his brow and he jerked his head sharply back, indicating that Kant should follow him to the back room. They slipped unnoticed from the bar, and into a tiny hallway, the door creaking shut upon the bawling crowd.

O'Shea gave the reporter a whispered explanation of what was happening, before they entered the back room.

'Mick is a master at hiding his worries,' he said.

A clock on the wall was showing the wrong time. It was

as round and blank as Collins' face, giving nothing away. He and the smartly dressed Mulcahy looked as though they were meeting as part of a business arrangement, while Brugha looked twitchy and unsure. Kant leaned back, made himself oblivious in the smoke and shadows.

In sharp contrast to Collins and Mulcahy, there was no trace of comfort in Brugha's clothing and appearance. His jacket was frayed at the edges, his shirt collar patched and worn out. His prominent eyes added to his scarecrow aspect. It struck Kant that Brugha's outfit had been as carefully chosen as Collins' soft grey business suit, the French shoes and the hat with its elegantly dented crown. Brugha intended to set an example of a revolutionary leader beyond reproach, one capable of financial discipline, even when luxuries were easily within reach.

Collins wore a generous smile to show that he had nothing to fear from their company. By contrast, Mulcahy looked sad and dutiful, as if at pains to show he was taking no pleasure in the meeting. He made no objection when Collins sent for a bottle of whiskey from the bar.

The IRA leader looked up at Mulcahy and said a few words in Irish in a tone of reproach.

'How are the new shoes, Mick?' replied Mulcahy. He had caught sight of Collins' expensive-looking footwear.

'They're pinching a little. Let's have a drink together Richard.'

'You've been avoiding us, Mick.' He began to draw patterns in the air with his fingers, but the movements were constricted and agitated, as though his hands were writhing against invisible chains.

'Dublin Castle has been hot on my heels. Where's your glass?'

'I'm off the hard stuff.' Mulcahy's fingers strained for greater freedom. 'These days it's better to keep a clear head.'

Collins shouted over his shoulder, 'Where's that bottle of whiskey?'

Brugha stepped forward. 'I've discovered some suspicious discrepancies in how you've been managing the IRA funds.'

Mulcahy watched the two men closely, his fingers moving faster, like delicate counting instruments.

Collins hit the table with the palm of his hand. 'A bottle of whiskey,' he shouted again. 'What's that Cathal?'

'I've found suspicious discrepancies in your accounts.'

'Suspicious? Don't we all know you're the most suspicious man in Ireland, Cathal. If your own mother walked through that door you'd think the British sent her.'

'I'm talking about expenses that can't be accounted for in the normal running of a war.' Brugha sat down without removing his crumpled coat.

'What are you running now, an accountancy firm?' asked Collins. He glanced at Mulcahy with a grin.

A waiter swung a bottle of whiskey onto the table. Collins was at pains to show his ease, with his left arm dangling over the back of his seat, and his right stretched out holding the bottle.

'Where's your bloody glass, Cathal?', he growled.

Mulcahy intervened. 'The leaders of Sinn Fein want to be reassured about the finances, Mick. The revolution is entering a whole new phase. We're preparing for self-government, to run the country. The high-spending days are over. We can't keep running around like footloose business-men throwing out favours at every turn.'

Collins stared at Mulcahy's moving hands, a bewildered frown erupting on his face, as though he had suddenly realised the power their owner possessed. 'I thought we were fighting a war, not squabbling about petty cash.'

Neither Mulcahy nor Brugha said anything in response. Collins looked at them as if to say, 'are you done?'

Brugha opened his briefcase and removed a thin envelope. 'This is an unofficial report I have compiled on your management of the National Loan. Next week I'll be handing it into the ruling council.' He placed it in front of Collins, who ripped it open and read its contents.

'Is that all you have against me?' he asked, throwing the letter onto the beer-stained table, his face going pale. He began to drum his feet upon the floorboards. Brugha pushed his seat backwards, while Mulcahy raised his playing fingers, like a priest fending off an attack with a blessing.

'You know nothing about running an army,' shouted Collins, rising to his feet. He brushed roughly against Brugha. 'For the last six months you've been waging a jealous vendetta against me, ever since I usurped your role as Minister of Defence. You've been trampling through my personal life, trying to sniff out scandal. And now you dare to call me an embezzler.' Blood spurted into his cheeks. 'You can't imagine the onerous burden it is to run the IRA's finances. Never in my life have I come across such cowardice, envy and meanness.' Spitting out a string of curses, he spun on his heels and barged out of the room, almost taking the door off its hinges in the process.

O'Shea grabbed the letter, his fingers shaking. He made a visible effort of pulling himself together as he read it. He dropped it back onto the table as though it were a ton weight.

'This scrap of paper will destroy Mick's career,' he warned in a low voice. 'You're accusing him of mishandling money, and worse, corruption. A volunteer could be shot for less.'

Even though Mick had left, Mulcahy and Brugha looked wary, as though they were still in the presence of the IRA leader's heated temper, his force, his capacity for violence. Brugha lifted up his briefcase and turned to leave. 'I've examined the most up-to-date figures for the National Loan,' he said. 'There are a number of entries I can't find an explanation for, and I'm not talking about £10 missing here, or another £50 there. I'm talking about large regular sums of money going missing. Mick has one week to supply me with the full accounts, including receipts, before the ruling council passes judgement.'

Mulcahy spoke with pale-faced civility. The authority in his voice and soft hands had returned. 'Mick should know that, if there are discrepancies in the accounting, the ruling council will investigate them with determination. We can't let this war be run with the mentality of men enjoying an unexpected windfall.'

When they had left, O'Shea poured Kant a glass of whiskey.

'I have made you privy to an explosive secret.'

'You have my word – I will tell no one.'

'Your promise must be sealed by more than words.'

Kant nodded. He had already surmised that O'Shea had invited him to the back room in order to secure his assistance.

'Brugha is nothing but a stooge for Dublin Castle,' explained O'Shea. 'They're to blame for this entire mess. British intelligence has been gathering a file on Mick's spending. They've been collecting receipts, investigating bank accounts, raiding offices.'

Kant frowned. 'Why are they so interested in his finances?'

'The file they are putting together is political poison. An

idea hatched by the Dirty Tricks Brigade. It paints a picture of embezzlement and corruption, millions of pounds flooding in from America, and Mick swept along on their tide.'

'What do they plan to do with the file?'

'They want to make him run.'

'To London?'

'And a peace settlement. It all fits together nicely for them. They want the charges of financial impropriety hanging over Collins so he'll do a deal quickly. They're threatening to ruin his reputation, and toss the shreds to the press and his enemies. It's been done before. Look at what happened to Parnell. The country turned against him when they discovered his affair. Nowadays, a leader accused of corruption will draw a similar public outrage. Brugha doesn't realise it, but he's fallen completely into their trap.'

'If Mick is innocent of these charges then he will be able to clear his name.'

'Unfortunately he can't. For once, he's unable to produce his meticulously prepared accounts. Earlier this year, the British seized an important set of financial documents and locked them away in Dublin Castle. They include the records Brugha is now querying. He expects every sixpence to be accounted for in spite of the raids. Poor Mick is at a loss as to how the money was spent. He won't be able to clear his name unless he finds the file.'

'Which is where I come in,' said Kant.

'Correct. I want you to retrieve the documents from Dublin Castle.'

'What if they are no longer there?'

'Then Mick is sunk, and the British will win the war. Do you have any reason to believe they're not there?'

He looked into O'Shea's eyes. He was not by nature an

untruthful man, and he wanted to tell the truth, that he suspected the documents either had been burnt or were sitting in the attic above his bedroom, but something about the agitated look in O'Shea's face made him hold back.

'No,' he said, looking him firmly in the eye. 'This is the first time I've heard of their existence.'

He was beginning to understand the magnitude of the file Lily Merrin had removed from the intelligence archive, and the reason why she had forced it upon him. He felt the deadweight of its political importance. God help her, he thought. She had not asked to have her and her son entangled in such a sinister plot, an enterprise hatched to derail the course of the war. It helped explain why she was still in hiding, lost, beyond help from Dublin Castle, General Stapleton and Mick Collins. It was hard to accept that none of them seemed to care about her plight, especially Collins. He didn't know for certain if the IRA leader had refined or altered his plans for her, or completely abandoned her.

The clock on the wall began to chime the hour. Kant looked up and saw that it was still showing the wrong time. The hands indicated 5 o'clock but it could only have been one or two at the most. Somehow, the mechanism was working but the hands were stuck. How long had they remained like that, he wondered. It was another intimation that he was in a world where things did not make sense, where rules and loyalties were casually abandoned. Perhaps Ireland was a country where order and allegiances never existed in the first place, where even the contraction of time and a mother's bravery were pointedly ignored by everyone.

SEVENTEEN

A dinner party was in full swing at Furry Park mansion when Kant mounted the steps to its main entrance. He glanced up at the looming flank of the east wing. Electric lights blazed from the conservatory, illuminating it like a glass cage, revealing a world of immaculately dressed men and women gliding about on a dance floor, sipping glasses of champagne under sparkling chandeliers, their faces absorbed, enraptured, oblivious of the looming dangers to their exalted way of life.

He rang the bell and waited. In the distance, the sea churned endlessly. A red-stockinged doorman answered his call, eyed him with suspicion, and took him into a little side room, where he was made to wait again.

He heard the sound of excited laughter in the hall, and then a slender hand carrying a cigarette in a long holder pushed opened the door. A tall, agile-looking woman appeared, wearing a brown, gold-brocaded frock with clinging sleeves. She was carefully groomed, with chiselled features. Her glistening eyes bore a look of disappointment when she saw the strange, hollow-faced visitor standing there, as though she had been expecting someone else.

At first, Kant thought one of the guests had strayed from the dinner party for a secret assignation. He quickly introduced himself as a reporter from the *Daily Mirror*, and watched her eyes turn hard and uninviting.

'What justification do you have for gate-crashing my party?'

'I must speak to Moya Llewelyn Davies urgently.'

'Must you, indeed', she replied sarcastically. From a dining room came the clatter of plates being stacked and chairs slithering back.

'I'm trying to find a missing woman called Lily Merrin.'

Her shoulders stiffened slightly. 'I am Lady Llewelyn Davies. What reason do you have to believe I might know the whereabouts of this woman?' She regarded him with a superior air, as though her presence might be enough to make him retreat and disappear back into the night.

Kant removed the letter about the widow's pension and flourished it in the air. 'I have evidence in this document that you assisted the Republican Army with their finances. You are obviously an acquaintance of Collins. Perhaps you can shed light on his involvement in this woman's disappearance.' Kant was careful not to suggest he was blackmailing her with the letter.

She flinched slightly and the look of suspicion deepened in her face.

'I'm surprised you think it's worthwhile troubling me with this matter. I might be a supporter of Mick Collins, but I'm not a kidnapper or a murderer.'

'Three women have died and another is missing, and so is her son. I don't know where they are, but I believe they are in grave danger. Every moment is precious. Which is why I have come directly to you with this letter, rather than report it to the authorities.'

'Is that a threat?' she said, taking the letter from him.

'No. I just want to speak to you in private. If you are busy, I can wait here.'

'That won't be necessary.'

Kant observed her as she read the letter, trying to glimpse beyond the unfriendly manner. He saw awkwardness and impatience, but little surprise or worry.

She gave him a level gaze. 'I hope you know what you're getting yourself into.' She walked back into the hallway. 'You'd better follow me upstairs. Away from my guests.'

A butler eyed Kant from the conservatory and turned up the volume on the gramophone player, as though the music was an instrument to blot out unwanted guests. Moya led him up a sweeping staircase and into a library, where she bid him sit on a luxuriously soft armchair.

She took a deep breath. 'I should really give a cove like you the marching orders. However, I'm concerned you might bring this letter with my incriminating signature to the authorities.'

'That is not my plan, at all.'

'Perhaps you are trying to trick me into some sort of confession. If my husband were here he would set the dogs upon you and have you horse-whipped, or worse.' She began to describe the cruel ways in which her husband, Crompton, the Solicitor-General to the post office, had chased off uninvited guests in the past.

'I just want to find out the importance of this letter'. Kant's chest wheezed as he spoke. 'It must be important because it has Mick Collins' signature and yours. But at the moment, it's meaningless to me.'

'I don't want to disappoint you, but it's meaningless to me as well. I haven't a clue what your letter is about. Mick is always sending me letters and cheques, and I sign them all without looking.'

'Does he coerce you into signing them?'

'No, not at all. I sign them out of boredom, to keep myself from falling prey to drinking or gambling.' She laughed and for the first time he realised that she was tipsy. 'My husband is busy in London, and things are very quiet this winter; you know, I'm attending only one dance a week.' Her eyes widened as her hand trailed through the air. Behind her upper-class veneer of superiority, he detected a recklessness, a willingness to flirt with the unmentionables of high society. He saw how a woman of her wealth, hopelessly exiled on such a lonely estate, would be susceptible to the dangerous charms of men like Collins. 'Here I am in this big old house full of servants with nothing to distract me. But thankfully, I've developed an interest in Irish politics. I've discovered there's something dangerous and addictive about being associated with Mick Collins, the most wanted man in Europe.'

Adventuresses, thought Kant. That was how the London press had labelled women like Moya, young, educated women who steeped themselves in political pamphlets, cut their hair and revoked their pampered upbringing for a revolutionary cause, and were ready to wallow in prison cells for their beliefs.

'A few months ago, I set up several bank accounts for Mick when all this money started coming in.' She sounded as though she was showing off her revolutionary credentials. 'There was so much cash flooding in from the fat accounts of Irish Americans, the IRA didn't know what to do with it. They'd have flushed it down the lavatory to keep Dublin Castle from getting their hands on it. As I'm the wife of a top British public official, Mick reckoned my accounts would be the last place they'd think of looking.'

'Aren't you concerned about what happens to the money

you're signing for, or where it's going? Aren't you afraid there might be a rotten apple in the IRA, squandering the funds?'

'Well it's kind of you to point that out to me. I'll certainly be more discreet about what I sign in future.' For a moment, her slightly inebriated air of superiority gave way to a look of schoolgirl adoration. 'To tell you the truth, the only cheque I'm afraid of signing for Mick is the blank one to my heart. Do you know why Mick is so successful in his war against the British?'

'No.'

'Because he has a modern vision of women's place in society. We belong to the centre of Mick's campaign, doing dangerous things, smuggling weapons, hiding bombs, stealing state secrets. This is why Dublin Castle has started hunting female rebels and murdering them. They feel threatened by us, by our burning convictions, our unwavering loyalty.'

'What dangerous things have you done?'

She eyed him carefully. 'I've done nothing dangerous.'

'Apart from signing letters and cheques you don't read. Are you afraid of becoming a hunted woman?'

'Is that what you've come here to talk about? I thought you wanted to find Lily Merrin.'

'I want to hear about your involvement in Mick's war. How he persuades women to do dangerous things. Women like you and Lily Merrin.'

'That's the crazy thing about the whole business with Lily,' she said with a smile. 'Mick didn't contact her, she contacted him. She wanted to strike a deal with him. The spying at Dublin Castle was based on mutual interest.'

What was she talking about, he thought. He felt an

unpleasant tightening in his chest. The look of discomfort in his face made her hesitate from any further explanation. He knew he should have spent a few more days recuperating in London. He'd exhausted all his strength in getting to Furry Park, and now he no longer had the energy to interrogate the tipsy wife of a senior government official, whose favourite pastime involved filling her salon with dangerous revolutionaries.

'Would you like a drink?' she asked. 'You look like you need a hot whiskey.'

An elderly servant brought him a brimming glass. The sweetness of the whiskey-scented air made his eyelids droop.

'Your letter and Merrin's disappearance are connected in one important way,' she told him. 'They're not about war or freedom. They're about money. The darkest and most urgent anxiety of our time.'

The music had stopped in the conservatory below, and the hallway echoed with the clicking of ladies' heels deserting the dance floor.

He tried to speak but another coughing fit took hold of him. He could smell the infection in his chest. He was ashamed to realise that everything about him reeked of sickness, his hoarse breathing, his pale face, the unsteadiness in his legs, his blurred vision. His fever was preventing him from seeing and hearing things clearly. He blinked to try to correct his vision. He got up to leave the room but stumbled. Everything went spinning and he fell back into his seat.

She rose calmly, adjusted her tight-fitting frock, and walked towards him.

'You smell like Mick,' she said.

'What do you mean?'

'I smell the whiff of a life on the run. The odour of backstreet boarding houses, trains, and dank cellars. The aroma of a fugitive.'

The heat of the room really was overpowering. A racking cough took hold of him, blunting his thinking, as though he were drunk. He stared at Moya, glassy-eyed, as she drew closer. His sudden weakness seemed to give her a more sympathetic face, her skin appearing softer, her eyes more penetrating. She muttered something and leaned towards him, looking deep into his burning eyes. Behind her elegant long eyelashes, there was no trace of fear or anger, just a cruel-looking amusement. His final thought before he slipped into unconsciousness was one of regret, that she had discovered his weakness before he could pinpoint hers.

EIGHTEEN

Collins had told Kant that the trick of a good spy was to hide in other people's secrets. It was a trick his survival now depended upon, he realised, when he awoke in a bed in a room with green print wallpaper. Without even stirring from his pillow, he sensed that he was being observed from the half-opened door. He was aware of the dim figure of Moya, and another shape joining her. At first, he thought it might be a doctor, summoned in the middle of the night to see him, but then he realised it was a woman, younger, dressed in a man's coat, her hair cropped and hidden under a broad-brimmed hat. She apologised for being late.

The figures of the two women hovered in the corridor. They talked and nodded together, snatches of their conversation drifting into his consciousness. His brain worked slowly with their words, trying to find the connections between the sentences.

'You should have set the dogs on him,' said the visitor. 'Or one of Mick's gunmen.'

'I had to let him in. It was a matter of courtesy.'

'If he was a gentleman, he'd have sought an invitation.'

'Make sure and barricade the door,' said Moya.

They stepped closer to his bed, whispering like conspirators. The presence of the other woman made him feel confused and suffocated. The gaslight dimmed. From the evidence of their shadows, he deduced they were conducting a thorough search of his clothes. Minutes passed, or perhaps much longer. He was not sure. A chill had supplanted his fever, making his teeth chatter, the infection burying itself deep in the roots of his lungs, making it painful to breathe.

'What are we meant to do with him?'

'It depends. Is he our patient or our prisoner?'

'Whatever he is, he's certainly not a detective.'

'I fear that he has managed to hit upon the truth.'

'I've never kept a man prisoner before.'

The visitor moved towards him. Her hair was dark and cut short, her face pale and delicate. She eyed him with a cool disregard. Kant felt a different kind of heat, something in his chest opening to desire and loss. He recognised her face, even though it was no longer framed by long hair. It was Lily Merrin.

He felt as though the bottom had dropped out of his bed. What sort of conspiracy had he stumbled upon, which juxtaposed an upper-class English hostess with a blackmailed secretary? He tried to fix his eyes on Merrin, but his gaze drifted. He wanted to hold onto the image of her face, in case she disappeared again, but the weight of his illness oppressed him. He knew she was about to vanish and he might forget that he had seen her. He was forgetting her already as she hovered over him. He fastened his gaze upon her eyes to stop himself slipping back into the torrent of his fever-ridden sleep. Why couldn't he stay awake, now that he had found her at last? But his efforts were to no avail, he felt himself plunge into unconsciousness.

He awoke with a hot, liquid headache. He tried to speak but every effort seemed countered by thick gravity. His lungs were not deep enough to summon up his next breath, and his eyes winced with the fever. He was relieved to find that the women were still there, whispering intently as if locked in an intimate dispute. They were studying a newspaper that was laid out on a table along with the contents of his wallet and the pension document.

'Whatever else Kant is, he's the first reporter to mention the women who went missing from Dublin Castle,' said Moya. 'All the rest peddle the same propaganda from the British authorities.'

'Then let him keep looking,' said Merrin. 'Maybe he'll find something interesting. We still want to know who murdered Dilly and Agatha.'

'He's not fit to look anywhere. Look how wasted he is.'

'You're right. He'll not learn anything in this state. Not for several days at least.'

'We'll have to put some meat on his bones.'

'He's dangerously ill.'

'When you don't worry about living you can see a lot more.'

He tried to hold back a coughing fit but it was like pressing one's fingers around a set grenade. When the fit came, it obliterated his thoughts completely.

'One of us will have to nurse him.'

'There is no end to these Englishmen.' Moya's voice sounded fainter, closer to the door. 'Their evil desires are limitless. Why should we save this one?'

'All men need a woman to chase. He's been following me since the afternoon we met in the hansom cab.'

'Someone was following Dilly and Agatha on the night they were murdered.'

Merrin noticed that he was awake and conscious. She

drew closer to him. He had never felt such attentive eyes.

'What do you know about me, Mr Kant?'

'Less than nothing,' he whispered.

'You're not telling me the truth.' She leaned closer. 'Where is the file I gave you?'

'I've kept it somewhere safe, like you said.'

'You were supposed to tell no one about it.'

'I kept my promise.'

'Then where did this letter come from.'

'A woman at Dublin Castle gave it to me.'

'One of Mick's women?'

'No. The unsuspecting wife of an informer.'

'Why have you held onto it? What is your motive?'

'My motive?' he asked. He wanted to say you are the motive, but his voice trailed away. He thought how unfair it would be if he died now, so close to finding out the secret of Merrin's disappearance, but his illness worsened, shutting down his faculties one by one. The fever rose like a fiery angel from his chest, swelling and filling the room, consuming the figures of the two women, the walls and the bed, until there was nothing left. He held onto the angel's ascending ankle, afraid of falling into the darkness forever.

NINETEEN

Lily Merrin's face ruffled the light from the heavy curtains. His startled eyeball fixed on her. It was morning and she had returned, her face dark and taut as she folded a set of cold compresses next to his bed. She was wearing a loose-fitting shirt tied with a belt and labourer's corduroy trousers, but he could sense the slender lines of her body beneath the sagging material. Why was she trying to fit into such an unwomanly disguise? And why was her hair cropped so short. Her outfit was a way of life, a uniform, he realised, nothing to do with convenience or her femininity; it announced a new vocation.

'You're fit enough to talk,' she remarked.

He'd been sweating heavily and his pillow was damp. He raised his head and tried to think, but he had no plots to set in motion, nothing else to consider but the look of wariness on her face, trying to read her, follow the flow of her thoughts.

'Yes,' he replied.

'Are you a detective sent by my mother-in-law?'

Her gaze was bleaker, her mouth harder than he remembered. Her expression reminded him of a predator's tenacity locking onto its victim. He closed his eyes, like an animal letting itself be dragged. He realised she had been dragging him ever since that soundless afternoon in the

191

hansom cab, her fingers touching his hair, her blind lips rushing towards his, finding their target, planting their seductive memories. She had dragged him the whole way across Dublin to this bedroom where the riddle of her disappearance now floated before him, coiling and shining, like a whip about to deliver its sting.

'No,' he answered eventually. 'How long have I been here?'

'Two days. Do you work for the Irish Constabulary?'

'No.'

'I don't believe you. You act like a detective, sniffing out clues. Who sent you?'

'General Stapleton. He was concerned for you. He wanted to find out why you had disappeared.'

'And what have you discovered?'

He closed his eyes, breathing heavily, seeking the camouflage of his illness, but she was determined to ransack his hiding places. She repeated the question. He kept his eyes closed but he was aware of the heat of her breath, the force of her presence.

'You have been playing a game,' he said hoarsely.

'Have you known my secret from the start?' She squinted at him, searching for a sign, but he hid it carefully and stared back at her with clouded eyes.

'No.'

'Do you know it now?'

'I have an inkling.'

A reporter needed special experience and insight to work out the true meaning of everything he had encountered since arriving in Ireland. He recalled the dank cellars of the castle, and Merrin's boarding house bedroom, the room full of billowing ashes, sooty flakes falling through the suffocating air. Revelations and understandings came to him at a speed he found difficult to contend with, like listening to an orchestra playing much too quickly. She had sealed herself up with her grief, he realised. Her entire story, as he knew it, was the invention of a mother coping with the worst form of separation imaginable. For a moment, she looked ready to unburden herself of her secret, to reveal the domestic crisis that had entangled her family life in a dangerous war.

'You know where I am hiding?'

'Not yet.'

'Then I will wait for you to find me.'

He closed his eyes, drowsed, slipped into a dream, woke again.

She was sitting at the bottom of his bed, talking about her husband, who had died at the Somme when their son was only five years old. She didn't seem to mind if he was awake or not.

'When I got the letter from the Ministry of Defence my whole world fell apart. His life was over and so was mine. The war went on, and everyone expected me to keep going, look after my son, run the family home, but inside I couldn't. I ignored my little boy, deserted my role as a mother. I became a shadow, all I wanted to do was disappear. They judged me, told me I was being selfish, that I should gather myself up and keep going. When I didn't pick up, they offered to take Isaac on holiday, but it was a trap, a chance for them to take him away from me forever. Only then did I realise that my son was all I had left.'

She rose from his bedside and pulled across the curtains.

'If I cease to be a mother, I cease to exist. They must know that.'

Light flooded the room, revealing her face in full detail, her skin, the movement of her lips.

'I will not permit him to be placed in harm's way,' she said. 'I am his mother and he is my son. I cannot abandon him now.'

'You reveal too much to me,' he said. 'There are spies everywhere. You should go now and keep your secret safe.'

She blushed slightly, and left the room, locking the door behind her. He heard her footsteps trail down a set of stairs and then disappear. With an enormous effort, he lifted his head , and then sank back onto the clammy pillow, resigning himself to sleep.

TWENTY

Kant's fever lasted another two days. He was unconscious for most of it, but his compressed moments of lucidity were long enough for him to develop deeper feelings towards Lily Merrin, who seemed to have made his recovery her special charge. He did not understand how he had attracted this mysterious bedside attendant. He felt her looming presence permanently in his subconscious, simultaneously easing his symptoms and interrogating him. And then abruptly, she disappeared, like the fever itself.

He awoke one morning to an empty room and a chill sense of loss. His temperature had come down, and the pain in his chest had disappeared, to be replaced by something less tangible, an uneasiness. Physically, he had not been better in years, but he felt somehow impoverished by good health, with only a superficial sense of healing, his emotions frustrated and strained rather than soothed. He felt the end of something, the fleetingness of a relationship between a patient and a nurse. He had always believed that making love was the most intense form of intimacy between a man and a woman. Now he realised that wasn't even the beginning. Illness was the culmination of intimacy, being looked after by someone as you hovered between life and death.

For the rest of the next day, he barely moved from the bed. A maid came and brought him food at intervals, but of

Lily Merrin and Moya, there was no sign. He drew a sense of comfort from the thought that he had battled his way through danger and illness to reach this temporary haven, a comfortable old bed in a room with a fire and a window with a view of manicured lawns leading down to the sea. However, it unsettled him to think that men like Collins and Isham were still going about their secret routines on the streets of Dublin.

He listened carefully to the noises of the house, the creaking of floorboards, the air wafting in currents and tides under the door, the fastening of doors and windows, the crumbs of soot falling into the fireplace in front of his bed. Sometimes, he thought he heard the sound of a boy playing in a distant room, testing the depth of silence with his laughter. He kept hoping for the footsteps of the women on the stairs, anticipating the return of their tenderness and subterfuge, feeling less like a patient and more like a prisoner guarded by two wayward ghosts.

On the fifth day, he awoke feeling sharp and extraordinarily alert. His recovery had given him a breathless sense of urgency, his heart beating with a violent desire to live. He saw everything in clear fragments, the Dublin of alleyways and backstreet boarding houses, the empty rooms filling with ashes, the meetings and conspiracies moving from one secret location to another, the daily shootings and ambushes, all had been a place to hide from living. For the first time in weeks, he no longer felt pain every time he breathed deeply.

After breakfast, he decided to get up and dress himself. His clothes had been washed and laundered. He lit the fire with birch logs from a neatly piled stack, and watched the flames lick hungrily at the dry bark. He poked through the wardrobe by his bed, ran his hand over the rack of clothing, the business suits belonging to a broad-shouldered man, dressing-gowns, double-cuffed shirts, a silver-tipped cane, expensive looking, and a pair of black leather gloves sitting on a shelf. He wondered who had been the last inhabitant of the room.

He listened to the comings and goings of servants. He stood in the centre of the room, breathing in the life that was stirring in the mansion, the tide of movement, the sense of order and hurry, footsteps going back and forth, but none with the light familiar tread of Lily Merrin.

Before lunch, he made his way down the stairs and through a hall lined with the horned heads of Irish deer and the smoky portraits of the mansion's former owners. He walked into a wide drawing room. He seemed to have the run of the place. He explored the other floors. The curtains were barely opened and the rooms were filled with a silky light, like the sheen of fresh snow. A spell seemed to have fallen upon everything, sheets of muslin covering the furniture, a great web claiming all the rooms while he had been sleeping.

An elderly servant dressed in black skirts led him down to the dining room for lunch. She seemed starved of company, and it was easy to draw her into conversation. He learned that Moya had left suddenly to spend the rest of winter with her husband in London. Her nerves have given way, again, she explained. 'She can't manage on her own,' she grumbled. 'The lady is forever closing the place down and opening it again on a whim. More a hobby than a great house.' Her face turned toward him out of the gloom. In her grey eyes, he caught sight of an interesting blend of wisdom and spite.

'I heard a boy playing while I lay in bed,' he said.

She scowled. 'The little varmint. He's forbidden to come near the house, especially when there are visitors.'

'It must be difficult, keeping a child confined in such a way.'

'You can never keep a child confined. Like troublesome little insects, they are.'

She scooped back the curtains, flooding the room with a blinding light.

'If I catch sight of him, I'll drag him by the ear back to his room,' she said.

She went off and brought him back his lunch. Kant was glad to see that, although the lady of the house had departed, the place did not go short of luxuries. The servant placed a meal of fresh mackerel and baked breads before him. When she returned to collect the plates, he asked her where the boy was staying.

'I'm not supposed to say,' she grumbled. 'There's a rumour going round that he's Mick Collins' illegitimate son.'

However, that was all she would divulge to the reporter. He bunched up his napkin in annoyance and walked through the ground-floor rooms but all he saw was more furniture draped in muslin and dustsheets. He felt the deadweight of secrecy, the vagueness and apathy that descend when living things are hidden away, and even familiar objects become invisible to each other.

He strolled through the grounds of the estate, and tried to work out a plan of action. He roamed across the manicured lawns. A black mood of impatience settled upon him. He was unsure of what Lily expected from him. Was he meant to wait silently for her next move or follow some trail of clues or secret signals? Unfortunately, he did not know where to begin his search. He explored the dark places of the estate, the conical tower of a folly, an abandoned church, a path through a dark plantation of firs, a block of stables and outhouses. Some of the doors opened, and frantic, twittering birds rushed towards him. Others were locked, and he strained to listen but could detect no signs of human life. He walked around the three-storeyed mansion, inspecting the ivy clambering around the casement windows, watching for a shadow at the glass or a movement. He trekked around a water-lilied lake, through banks of rhododendron and over wintering shrubs. An empty mansion and its privileged domain of lawns and specimen trees on a December afternoon. This was all he could see. Nothing less, nothing more.

Her appearance in the bedroom had filled him with conviction. She had come to his side, deliberately this time. She had singled him out and the realisation filled him with caution. She had given him a part to play in her mysterious disappearance, but it was beyond his power to divine its exact nature or alter it in any way. He walked through the mansion, scrutinising the veiled furniture, the silence of the abandoned rooms, waiting uneasily for a sign to reveal itself. He returned to the dining room, with its conservatory views of the pine forest and in the distance, a restless sea.

About an hour later, something woke him. He opened the French doors, telling himself to stay alert. It was late afternoon, and he had the sense that something about the estate had changed, a heavy hidden presence that had not been there before, the sense of something menacing sharpening the air.

He walked towards the block of outhouses. A dog began barking. He could hear voices, footfalls, the sound of wood splintering. He hurried through a wide-arched entryway into the stable courtyard. The noises were emanating from behind one of the locked doors.

He battered the door with his fist. 'Lily, are you there?'

The noises stopped. He placed his eye against the rusted keyhole and peered into the dusty darkness. The door fell open, knocking him off balance. Before him stood the tall figure of Isham in a riding jacket, jangling a set of keys in his hand.

'The keys, Kant. Before you conduct a search, always obtain the keys first.'

The reporter stumbled backwards.

'You don't look too happy,' said Isham. 'You should be relieved to see me. I've brought the cavalry to your aid.'

Behind him, a group of soldiers were upending the bric-a-brac, rusty farming implements, old rowing boats, horse's tack draped in scarves of dusty cobwebs. They drove their bayonets deep into piles of hay and straw, and sacks of old seed potatoes, sending up a pall of dust and decay. A colony of dead mice fell from a split sack like a soft grey intestine. Through a dusty window, Kant caught sight of another lorry load of soldiers arriving.

Isham's face was cold and placid, his eyes empty.

'Where is Merrin?' he demanded.

'I don't know. I presume somewhere as far away from here as possible.'

Isham stared at Kant in silence. 'I want more than that. I hope you will see sense and give me more than that.'

'Sorry, I don't think I can.'

'I received a tip-off from one of Collins' men that you were hot on Merrin's trail, and he sent you here. I hear that Collins doesn't quite know what to do with you, and I sympathise with his dilemma. Here you are, a prying reporter pretending to be a spy, a professional shadow, and a confidant to everyone, who won't give up his pursuit of a double-crossing secretary. I can't go on protecting you from yourself and your weakness for this woman. It's time you allowed the professionals to take over.'

'I was close to solving the riddle of her disappearance, but I fell ill. I've been confined to bed for the past four days. She came to my bedside and interrogated me. She wanted to know who sent me. I've recuperated enough to mount a search of the grounds this morning, but I can't find any trace of her at all.'

'What did she confide in you?'

'Practically nothing.'

'I don't believe you. Women talk. They always talk. They like to find a confidant. What did she tell you?'

'I've already told you. Almost nothing.'

'Who is Mick hiding her from?'

'Dublin Castle and her mother-in-law.'

'Who else is she hiding from?'

'I didn't get the feeling there was anyone else.'

'She must have confided in you. Told you about her enemies.'

The use of the plural intrigued Kant.

'Who has been posting her letters?'

'Writing letters has been the last thing on her mind, I presume.'

'What about postcards. Surely there was someone to deliver her messages?'

'I don't know. I wasn't fit to keep her under surveillance.'

'Did she ask you to post anything for her?'

'No.'

'Your denials come very easily.'

'Because they're true.'

'She must have told you about her enemies.'

The glint in his eyes opened up a new labyrinth for Kant. What enemies was he talking about? Who else had Lily been hiding from? He wondered had she a lover, someone else she might have betrayed.

Isham studied him carefully. 'You seem as much in the dark as the rest of us.' He paused. 'Very well, you are at liberty to continue your search for Merrin. I'll assign several of my men to help you.'

'I work better on my own.'

'Have it your own way then.' He looked up at the empty mansion. 'I fear she has already flown the nest.'

More of Isham's men invaded the stables, ransacking the place with diligence and vigour. Their soldierly sense of calm, as though this was all a training exercise, helped Kant past the momentary panic. He detached himself from the search and made his way back to the house. A wave of desperation washed over him, the fear that he was never going to find Merrin, that the odds were stacked too heavily against him. Perhaps it was time to stop living within the memory of something that never really existed, a relationship with a mysterious woman based on little more than a coincidence and a single kiss. No matter how much he searched, he feared he would end up a lonely figure, condemned and lost, as he was now, wandering across an expanse of lawn where even the cold winter wind passed through him, looking for something else.

A shadow at the corner of his vision snagged his attention. The fleeing figure of the elderly maid. She was carrying a small suitcase and hurrying with conviction into the dark plantation of fir trees. He was surprised how swiftly she was moving, her great black skirts flaring and flapping against the wind-tossed shimmer of the pine needles. Making sure that no one was following him, he set off in pursuit.

The wind was as noisy as the Atlantic in the plantation. He followed her along a tortuous path that led to the sea. Above them, the tips of the fir trees almost blotted out the sky. The rough ground was hard with frost, and his ears rang with the cold, drowning out the roar of the trees. Eventually, a hole of blue opened ahead, and they came out at a hidden bay and a cottage fitting snugly into a corner of the rugged coastline. The tide was fully in, and the wind was whipping the watery light over the coastline, giving everything a wild stunned look, as though a thunderstorm had unloaded its static from the sky.

Some hens flew off, startled, as the maid entered the front yard of the cottage. She knocked on the door, called out against the wind and the door opened promptly.

The woman at the door seemed unprepared for guests. She curled inwards when she saw Kant appear behind the maid, collapsing back into the darkness. She had not been expecting him to drop in like this, that much was clear. He followed her into the darkness of a tiny front room, barely lit by a smouldering turf-fire. Even though he had recovered from his fever, he felt out of his depth, unsteady on his feet. He watched Lily Merrin recover her poise, straighten up, smooth the long plain dress she was wearing.

TWENTY-ONE

The sea hissed at the window of the hushed cottage. The sill was filled with speckled shells, pebbles glinting like gems, gnarled pieces of rope and driftwood, the little knick-knacks a mother and son would gather from a beach.

'Where's Isaac?' asked Kant.

'I've sent him to stay with a relative I can trust,' replied Lily.

'You must leave now. You don't have any time.'

He stepped towards her so that she was squeezed against the smoking fire.

'It's true miss,' said the maid. 'The soldiers are searching everywhere.' She opened the suitcase and began packing Merrin's clothes from a wardrobe. Kant moved closer to Merrin, as though she was a wild creature in need of protection. Even in the dim light, he could see the fugitive gleam in her eyes.

'I wasn't meant to kiss you that afternoon, or give you the file,' she said. 'That wasn't part of the plan. Our paths were never meant to cross.'

'Part of what plan?'

She stepped to the side and stood against a door leading to a back room. She smiled at him, knowing that she had frustrated his attempt to close down her escape routes.

'Please,' she said, pushing a chair towards him. 'Listen to the story that I have to tell.'

'I don't want to hear it. You don't have any time.'

'You should hear the truth.'

Reluctantly, he sat down. 'I've already guessed.'

'You can go, now,' Lily commanded the maid, then she turned to Kant. 'You still have the file?'

'You don't understand, Lily. I don't want to hear about the file. I'm here to warn you that you don't have much time. You've got to get away.'

She loomed closer. Her short hair made her eyes seem larger.

'The moment I kissed you, I cursed us both.'

She was so close he could smell the peppermint smell of her skin. He had to lean back to look at her properly, and what he saw was not the face and eyes of his memory, the stricken features that had fed his imagination for the past fortnight. What he saw was confirmation that she was no longer the mysterious woman suffering an inexplicable family tragedy. She had grown similar to him. Her proximity stilled the panic in his heart, and prompted him to take a risky plunge into the unknown.

'In the circumstances, being cursed is neither here nor there. It belongs to another world. I don't care about the trouble you have brought upon yourself, or upon me. I'm just asking you to leave with me now. We can catch the next boat to England. It will be easy to make a fresh start. Your boy can join us in London. At least for a year or two until things have improved in Ireland. There'll be a political solution soon to all this fighting and treachery. I'll arrange somewhere for you to stay, help you find a job.'

Her face tightened. 'Thanks for the offer, but it won't solve anything. There's no escape plan you can come up with that I haven't gone over in my head dozens of times.'

'Then what do you intend to do? You can't just wait here to be arrested.' He told himself that she was stunned by fear and that when she collected her thoughts she would realise and accept that he was rescuing her.

'There are still things you don't know about me.'

'What things don't I know?'

'For a start, you don't know how I met Michael Collins or how he saved me from despair. You think it's you who's been searching for me, that you came to Furry Park by your own powers of detection. You're wrong. I've been following you for the past fortnight, trying to work out if I can trust you or not. You were a mystery to me, why you were in the cab that day, whose side were you on? I followed you to the pub the night you met General Stapleton and his ring of spies. I watched Mick and his men drag you to the train station. I left the bar in Vaughn's Hotel, a moment before you and Mick entered. And it was me that convinced Moya to let you recuperate in the safety of Furry Park, rather than throw you back to Mick and his henchmen.'

As she recounted her story, Kant remembered the lightness and fear in her first caress. He realised that he had lived too long in the solitary confinement of his illness, shunning company, until that fateful afternoon when a strange woman's voice and caress became a web, and her kiss a spider bite. She spoke at length, staring not at Kant, but into the fire, at something private and painful.

'The IRA kidnapped Isaac, but they were acting under my instructions,' she told him. 'His disappearance was engineered to look like an abduction, but really they were rescuing him. Last year, my mother-in-law took custody of him, claiming I was an unfit mother. She has no respect for the natural laws of family life, that a son should be with his mother.'

'What made you trust Collins and his henchmen to do such a thing?'

'They have a code of honour.' She raised her chin. 'It may not be the same as yours, but it is the reason why ordinary Irish men and women entrust them with their future. All I had to do was keep my side of the bargain, and smuggle out certain documents from Dublin Castle. Mick and I arranged it all one winter afternoon in an hotel sunroom overlooking the sea.'

'But that amounted to betrayal. You handed over secrets that placed men's lives in jeopardy.'

'Don't talk to me about betrayal. You will never understand the betrayal a mother feels when she is deprived of her son. Please don't mention that word again.'

'What about the courts? You could have taken legal action. Pressure could have been applied to your mother-in-law in all sorts of ways.'

'The courts would have dragged the case out for months, years even. Time that I would never get back with my son. My options were limited. Abandon my son to my monstrous mother-in-law, or trust in the slow and indecisive justice system. The first was unacceptable. I agonised over the decision for weeks.'

Kant dropped the line of questioning. The agony of her separation was a formidable emotional obstacle, impossible to scale by logic or reasoning.

'And what about you?' asked Merrin. 'You've yet to tell me why you were in the hansom cab that afternoon.'

'Very well, let me confess. I've known more about your case than anyone else in Dublin Castle. My connection with it began in London, through a *Daily Mirror* colleague who wrote the initial reports about your son's disappearance. He confided in me your mother-in-law's suspicions that you might know something about Isaac's whereabouts. He thought it would make a more interesting story, a front-page headline, but all he had to work on were the misgivings of your mother-in-law. He asked me to follow you while I was in Dublin. Unfortunately for him, I'm not a very good detective or a spy either. Our paths crossed, something passed between us, and from that moment I haven't been the same.'

'Not the same as what?'

'I mean I was no longer myself. A reporter dabbling in the dangerous game of propaganda and spying. I became your servant, linked to you for ever, not by your kiss or your touch, but by the certainty that we were both operating alone, abandoned by fate to a city teeming with crooks and murderers.'

For a moment, she appeared to relax, as though acknowledging there was no longer any need for secrecy or deception. He needed stronger confirmation of her feelings, so he grabbed her hands. He wasn't afraid of bruising her. She yielded under his pressure. She understood his need, even though her hands were limp, boneless almost. He held her hands so tightly she couldn't grip back, but her face and eyes welled towards him, as though mentally she was reaching out towards him. He wanted more from her so he pressed himself closer. Alarm flashed across her face. For a moment, he wondered had he miscalculated, misread her signals. She shrunk back, her eyes blooming with fear. She wasn't looking at him, he realised. She was staring through the window, at a grey horse standing motionless in the front yard.

The front door of the cottage shook. A sharp blow struck it and a chink of light flooded in. The bottom half of the door caved in and then the top. The figure of Isham shouldered his way into the cottage holding the butt of the rifle he had used as a battering ram. At a remove behind him stood a row of soldiers, their guns raised ready to fire.

TWENTY-TWO

The arrest of Lily Merrin was a sad little ceremony. Two soldiers led her out with rifles raised. Now that she was a prisoner, she looked transformed, remote and almost unapproachable, a peasant shawl draped about her head as she carried her small suitcase of belongings. The wind tossed her shawl, screening her face, so that Kant was unable to see what expression she was wearing.

General Stapleton had arrived in a military car. He stood respectfully at the threshold, as though he were making a formal visit to the cottage. He looked reluctant to enter and examine Merrin's hiding-place, as though it involved crossing a frontier to a dark, rebellious country. He turned smartly, saluted Isham, and conferred briefly with each of the soldiers, barely acknowledging the silhouette of Kant, who was kneeling on the ground.

Under Isham's interrogation, Kant tried to avoid revealing what he knew about the kidnap plot involving Merrin's son. With a fiendish look on his face, Isham took out his gun and raised it to the reporter's temple.

Kant kept his mouth shut and wondered, when Isham squeezed the trigger, why the hammer had not moved. The gun was only on half-cock, he realised.

'This is the last time you play this game of secrecy with the British Army, sir,' Isham warned him as he pulled the hammer back a notch, and levelled the gun again at the reporter's head.

Kant listened to the sound of his heart beating in his chest. Although his body was weak, his heart felt strong and warm. He wondered what would happen to Merrin now that she had been arrested. He felt a generous burst of blood fill his veins at the thought of her vulnerability as a prisoner. It struck him that she needed his protection more than ever. He stared at Isham's face, but he didn't see the corporal. His gaze was inward, imagining the terrible dangers Merrin might face in Dublin Castle. At the risk of losing all, Kant gave in, and reluctantly briefed Isham and the general on the story he had gleaned from Merrin.

When he had finished, Stapleton merely hesitated, as if conscious that a rebuke or threat was required, but all he gave Kant was a brief look of confusion. The reporter knew that, as far as the general was concerned, he no longer existed. Stapleton climbed into his car and sped off. His abrupt departure left Kant feeling more like a sacked employee, an unwanted visitor, a man whose role and name belonged to darkness.

Isham mounted his horse, and nudged the beast towards Kant, who was still kneeling.

'You deserve my most heartfelt congratulations,' said the corporal, his face wearing a look of undisguised contempt. 'For a man who looks as though he lives only on memories and remorse, you have a special talent. I knew if I left you to your own devices you'd bring me her head on a platter.'

'I did what I was told to do,' said Kant, climbing stiffly to his feet. 'Find Lily Merrin with a minimum of fuss.'

'You should have told Dublin Castle about your plans to search Furry Park. You should have sought assistance and advice.' The horse nosed towards Kant, looming with its velvety nostrils, inspecting the reporter's smell, before jerking back its head and neck.

'I hadn't time to tell anyone else.'

The look of scorn deepened on Isham's face. 'You haven't been thinking straight. You went about your job with the mentality of an amateur, and there's nothing Collins likes more than crushing amateurs.' His horse wheeled round with abrupt, reckless strength. The corporal held out his left rein and swung the animal back into position. 'Collins has been playing a complicated game of chess with you right from the start, forcing you into positions where the only move you could make got you deeper into trouble. Time after time until the inevitable checkmate arrived. That's what happened to your search for Merrin. Once you made the original error of assuming Collins' men had kidnapped the boy to blackmail her into spying, you made a series of unavoidable moves that could have ruined Dublin Castle's intelligence effort. Your short-sightedness could have led to your death and jeopardised the lives of others.'

'I don't understand why Collins allowed me to continue with the misapprehensions in the first place.'

'It was to keep our noses out of his business.'

'And what business is that?' asked Kant, thinking of Collins' secret bank accounts and his countless notebooks.

'The business of war, of course.' Isham tightened the reins and prepared to set his horse off into a canter. 'Collins was never interested in peace negotiations with Stapleton or any form of compromise. My informers tell me he's planning an all-out war against England, including a bombing campaign on the mainland. Innocent civilians will be killed, but that is of no interest to these ruthless Irish rebels.'

He gave his horse a crack of the whip and sent it off on a galloping bolt along the beach, its hooves adding to the leaping sea spray. Kant watched until they were a tiny shadow stirring the stillness of the horizon. He made his own way back through the plantation of fir trees, breathing in deeply the cold pine scent, as though he were a man suddenly freed of an obsession, with duties to no one but himself. However, in reality, a deeper, more unsettling feeling had taken hold of him – the fear that Isham was correct, and that he had been sleepwalking through the streets of Dublin while Collins had been crystallising a plot more complicated and violent than even Dublin Castle could invent. Above all, he had the nagging dread that, now Merrin was a prisoner, her life was under threat like never before. He thought of his day as a bad dream that still held dreaded events in store.

Back in his boarding house room, he stood at the window overlooking a street filling with marching soldiers and the dirty slick of sleet. He could hear the mournful shunt of trams carrying their passengers home. Metallic grit and soot mingled with the snowflakes and formed a dark web of melting ice on the glass. He wished he could wipe it clean, and see everything clearly, but his breath formed a layer of mist, obscuring his view further. Dublin was so filthy, the dark trams and horse-drawn carriages moving slowly, everything painted black to hide the grime. Even the uniforms of the policemen and soldiers passing in patrols were sullied-looking, a grubby camouflage merging with the foul streets. He wanted a dawn of unimaginable light to flood the city and rid it of the black melancholy of which he had been a prisoner for far too long.

It grew dark in the room. He turned, feeling how stiff his neck had grown from the stillness. He lit a gas lamp and rolling back the carpet, removed the file of papers from its hiding place. He stared at the file for a while without opening it. He felt troubled by his own stupidity. Gone was the feeling of excitement at his powers of deduction and pursuit. Instead he'd launched a clumsy attempt to rescue a woman who had been the architect of her own disappearance, a willing hostage to the IRA. Somehow he'd forgotten his place in this little war, blurred his allegiances, said the wrong words, became snared in the wrong narrative. He felt embarrassed that General Stapleton had witnessed the fiasco at the cottage. He tried to think with a new clarity, but all he could see was a deeper darkness within himself. The darkness of a man adrift in a city full of conspiracies, with no bonds of loyalty, and no plans as to how to extricate himself from the mess.

He lifted the file and it occurred to him that, if there was a way to comprehend the forces that had gathered around him, it might lie within its black leather covers. He studied the papers, this time with Isham's warning ringing in his ears. *It was to keep our noses out of his business. The business of war.* He read down the list of names, and thought what if they weren't the names of women, but something else, something that was necessary for an all-out war with England, a bombing campaign on the mainland? What if they were the names of chartered boats, and the dates not secret assignations but the sailing times across the Irish Sea?

His thoughts were interrupted by a gentle tap on the

door, followed by a whisper in a thick Dublin accent. 'Are you in, Mr Kant, sir?'

Kant put the file back under the floorboards and rolled out the carpet.

'Yes?' he said. He opened the door slightly. He didn't wish to examine his visitors too closely, but what he could see in the dim light of the landing was two men dressed in sharp business suits, their hair combed straight back, eyes simmering with a dangerous light.

'Where have you been, sir? We've been looking everywhere for you since Thursday.'

He searched the dark perimeter of their faces. 'Sorry,' was all he could manage to say.

'I should think so,' said the leader of the pair. 'You've overrun your account with Mr Collins.' There was something black and fat weighing down his hand. He jolted the door open with his boot.

'We'd almost given up on you,' he said, his voice expressing exasperation. 'Mick will not go easy on you. He hates Englishmen who break the rules.'

'He has rules then in his line of business?'

A passing train made a noise like a barrage of typewriters, their keys battering away automatically.

'Oh yes, sir. Englishmen must not outstay their welcome. That's definitely a rule of his.'

'I was detained at Furry Park. Where's Mick? I've something I need to discuss with him. Urgently.'

'A little patience, sir. You'll have your visit with Mick.'

He checked the pockets of Kant's jacket and trousers, ran his hands along the lining. They conferred with each other.

'What sort of spy goes about with empty pockets?'

'Mick said he was unhinged.'

'This way, I don't have anything to lose,' explained Kant.
'Everyone has something to lose in Dublin, Mr Kant.
Even the poorest man can gamble on his life. What you
mean to say is you are trying to avoid further losses.'

Without preamble, he struck Kant in the side of the ribs
with his fist. The blow made the reporter double over in
pain. He tensed his body, waiting for the series of blows
following each other in quick succession, but none came.
He was aware only of his wheezy breathing coming in slow
gasps. He took in a deep breath and straightened up. The
pain of the blow settled deep in his chest, supplanting the
habitual ache in his lungs.

'I was ordered to bring you with a minimum of fuss,'
said his assailant, his face close enough to smell the
alcohol and cologne. 'In my book that means the two of us
carrying you out, one at the head, the other at the feet. Of
course, you could save us the bother of bringing you out
unconscious.'

Kant nodded, mechanically. It wasn't fear of being struck
again that made him agree, just the realisation that it would
be entirely pointless to refuse. The first punch had been an
indispensable formality, their calling card. The henchmen
shoved Kant out the door and down the stairs.

A sense of solemnity had fallen on the deserted streets.
They hurried through the wet snow, carving out a path on
the thinly crusted cobblestones. Kant felt a rush of fear as
though they were descending a mineshaft into a deeper
darkness.

They stopped at a bridge over the Liffey. For a moment,
he believed they were going to tip him into the swirling
waters like a bagful of incriminating evidence, but then the
lights of a car swept through the falling snow and centred

their blaze upon the three of them. They lifted their hands to shield their eyes. The engine of the vehicle stopped and a door swung open. The henchmen grabbed Kant and pushed him blindly towards the light. He felt the metal of the car and reached for the door. A familiar face loomed up at him from the rear seat, a smile twitching the corners of his mouth.

'Climb in, Mr Kant,' said O'Shea.

The reporter sank into the seat beside him, letting his wet head fall back on the leather upholstery. The car slid into first gear, and he felt himself scooped up and whisked away from danger.

'I sense your despair, Mr Kant.' O'Shea wore an intent expression on his face. 'Desperate men make reckless decisions, which means risk, and there is always a financial danger when one encounters risk. As a life assurance manager, it is my job to reduce risk. Which is why I have organised this little trip with you.'

TWENTY-THREE

The car accelerated over cobblestones, taking the uneven road in easy style, its engine a silken purr. From his low seat, sheathed behind glass and insulating upholstery, Kant could not escape the feeling that he had crawled into a very sleek and expensive trap. Black curtains were drawn, shielding him and O'Shea from the chauffeur.

'I didn't know the IRA ran cars like this,' he said.

O'Shea shook his head. 'Not the IRA, Mr Kant. The vehicle belongs to me.'

Kant was impressed. 'The insurance business must be a good thing to have going.'

O'Shea smiled. He glanced at Kant's threadbare coat, his worn shoes. 'You might say I'm the only one to have a good thing going in Dublin at the moment.'

'Then you should get out while you're ahead. From what I hear, Mick is planning an all-out war. There'll be destruction and chaos.'

O'Shea's eyes glinted. 'Money is my obsession, not war, or freedom. How to get money and get it quickly. And right now I'm sitting on a sizeable fortune.'

'Wrong. You're sitting in the middle of a dangerous revolution.'

O'Shea's smile broadened. He began talking to Kant in the patronising way an adult talks to a child when something unpleasant is about to happen, regaling him with distracting details.

'These days there's a handsome profit in helping freedom-fighters, don't you know? Revolutions are the next big thing. Without large sums of money they're just a load of hot air, like that piece of theatrical buffoonery that was the Easter Rising. Underground movements need money just like a body needs blood. How else are they to organise meeting places, safe houses, propaganda and weapons, and train their fighters?'

Kant's head was still ringing from the cold, and it took all his concentration to comprehend what O'Shea was talking about.

'I didn't know there was a profit in a guerrilla war.'

'Not profit, Mr Kant, financial opportunity. When Mick recruited me to help raise finances, the volunteers were living on church collections. Practically begging on the street for money. I introduced a more systematic approach, and Mick put me in charge of fundraising. I began by squeezing money from fat-headed farmers and shopkeepers. Then we signed up the merchants and professional classes to shell out several times a year. We took advantage of their patriotic benevolence. Suddenly we had raised tens of thousands of pounds. But I didn't stop there.'

Kant nodded to keep up his side of the conversation.

'I'm a money-spinner, you see, not a patriot. I built up the National Loan from a glorified street collection for prisoners to a sum worth several fortunes. I saw it as my right to access a little of that money. I rerouted my cut to a little bank in London and invested the money. Made a fortune then lost it. Fortunately, for me, the revolution was providing a steady stream of revenue. As chief fundraiser,

I began to employ more effective methods at finding new sources of money. It's surprising how easy it is to take money off people when they believe it's a worthy cause. We screwed several widows out of their legacies, swindled money from large companies in the US. Big money, I'm talking about. All it took was a few accounting tricks to siphon off the funds from beneath Collins' nose. He and his comrades were always on the prowl for guns, throwing money around faster than gamblers dealing out hands of cards. The IRA's ruling council are revolutionaries, risk-takers, not the sort of men to hold on tightly to the purse strings. Especially the strings of a very large purse.'

'Why aren't you on the run? Or at least keeping a low profile. Instead of driving around in a chauffeur driven car like this.'

'A very pertinent question, Mr Kant. I've come to offer you help. Isham tells me you're going round in circles.'

'I wouldn't believe anything he says.'

'Quite right. You're not paying him to talk, and I am. Isham works for me. And no one else. Not the British Crown or Mick Collins. I selected him because he was ideally placed in Dublin Castle to make sure British Intelligence didn't get a whiff of my money-making enterprise.'

'Why are you telling me this?'

'Because it is in our mutual interest to stop Isham.'

'And why is that?'

'Lily Merrin.'

'What about her?'

'Isham murdered Susan O'Brien after she was arrested and brought to Dublin Castle, and he'll murder Lily Merrin in the exact same way, unless he's stopped. I dread to think how many other bodies he has hidden away.'

'What was your interest in Susan O'Brien?'

'Like everything else, it began as a matter of finance. She had willed her house, her entire fortune to the National Loan. All her silver, her paintings, even her jewellery. Unfortunately, her loyalty did not stop there. She got herself arrested for helping the IRA. Do you know what being found guilty of treason would have meant for her legacy?'

'No.'

'Everything would have been confiscated and auctioned by His Majesty. Knowing this, the only prudent course of action was to organise her escape before the charges could be brought against her.'

'And then her murder.' A shudder ran through Kant.

O'Shea's brows lowered over his eyes. 'I didn't pay Isham to kill her. That was his own solution to the problem.'

'What did he have to gain from murdering her?'

'Nothing. Greed is a very overrated motive for murder. The secrets of the human heart are much more powerful, in my experience.'

'And what are the secrets of Isham's heart?'

'Envy and lust. Isham was profoundly jealous of Collins and the unswerving loyalty of his female counterparts.'

'Collins and Isham are love rivals?' Kant raised his eyebrows.

'Surprised?'

'Not really. Crimes of passion happen all the time.' If Kant was surprised it was more because of the incriminating nature of the secrets O'Shea was confiding.

'Susan O'Brien's loyalty to Collins humiliated Isham. It was stronger than her wish to live. Can you imagine devotion like that?' A thin smile spread on O'Shea's lips. 'In Isham's eyes, she deserved to be punished. Just like the other female volunteers. Their weakness was their overriding belief that Collins could rescue them from any trap. That he could be bothered to spring them from a cell in the heart of Dublin Castle. As if he were their knight in shining armour. That was their only flaw. Loving him without question. They walked right out of Dublin Castle, expecting Collins to be waiting with open arms.'

'And instead they got Isham?'

'Correct.' O'Shea's grin tightened.

The car picked up speed, swooping through the empty streets. He caught its reflection in shop windows, gleaming like a royal carriage.

'I want you to be open with me as I have been with you.' O'Shea poked Kant in the ribs to get a response.

'Of course.'

'You found Merrin first. You talked to her before Isham arrested her. Did she tell you where she'd hidden the file she smuggled from Dublin Castle?'

Kant took a moment to absorb this new direction in their conversation. Now he began to understand why O'Shea was so keen to share his secrets with him. It was a bid to gain his trust and find out exactly what he knew about something that was much more important than Isham or the safety of Merrin.

'No,' he replied.

'Did she talk about what the file contained? Bank transactions, dates, signatures, anything like that?' Tension clouded his eyes.

'No. Why is the file so important to you?'

'It includes Mick's missing accounts, but the only person they'll incriminate is me. The list of numbers, they're bank transactions. They include orders to send IRA funds to my secret London accounts. When I heard Brugha was investigating all of the accounts, I knew it was only a matter of time before he discovered my little swindle. So I organised for Mick's offices to be raided by Dublin Castle and the incriminating accounts locked away in the British intelligence archive. Isham was meant to destroy the file in a fire at Dublin Castle.'

'But Merrin took it first.'

'My first and only piece of bad luck.' O'Shea's voice grew agitated. 'The missing file threatened to unravel everything. The fictitious banks, the fraudulent accounts. All my little games with numbers.'

'But you weren't unlucky. You were dishonest. You're a corrupt and greedy man, who's prepared to gamble a nation's legacy. You risked the downfall of better men, a country fighting for independence.'

'On the contrary, I think in hindsight people will realise I saved Ireland from a more bloody war. Without my financial tricks, the IRA would have bought a lot more guns and bombs. Look at Collins, his panic over the missing money almost propelled him into peace talks with the British. Future generations will be glad that I swindled him out of so much money. In fact you could almost say it was my patriotic duty.'

The car slowed smoothly to a stop. Its broad nose pointed at the dark fortress of Dublin Castle.

O'Shea had quelled his agitation. A half-smile reappeared on his lips. 'We're here, Mr Kant. Your lady friend is locked somewhere in the castle's dank cellars. Find her quickly before Isham does. Before he has her released and murdered.' He seemed anxious to be off, as though he had another piece of business to take care of, and didn't want Kant interfering with it.

After the car had driven away the entire city fell silent. Sleet fell in columns, pressing in upon the towers and battlements of Dublin Castle. Kant crossed the empty square, a shawl of melting flakes clinging to his head and shoulders. The silence added urgency to his fears for Merrin.

A single gaslight fluttered within the prison entrance. The place smelt like a decaying mausoleum and had a similar air of darkness and grief. He produced his security pass and made himself known to the guard on duty.

'Where's Lily Merrin?'

'Corporal Isham interrogated her earlier. She's back in her cell. Number 26. General Stapleton is still in his office upstairs. Do you wish to speak to him?'

'I'd rather not involve him right now,' he explained.

The guard conferred with his superior in a back office, then he pulled back the iron security doors and ushered Kant through.

A shadowy arch led into what felt more like a damp crevice running under tons of rock. The prison corridors seemed dark and convoluted but they carried their own reasoning. Death had been woven into the architecture of the castle; the more constricted the space, the closer one was to mortality. He descended a steep spiral staircase and found cell number 26. The door lay slightly ajar. He called out Lily's name, but there was no reply. The cell lay empty apart from a pool of shadows. He almost felt the floor open beneath him, so strong was the sinking sense of dread in his chest.

TWENTY-FOUR

It was snowing more heavily outside the castle walls. Kant kept walking, putting the dark fortress behind him, and all its secret relationships and conspiracies. He followed the snow as if hypnotised, all the way down its straight white line. His mind had reached a purer state, driven on by the cruelty of Isham's plot.

The temperature plummeted and the snow fell with greater intensity. He leaned into the cold, his mind searching through all the dead-ends, the false leads and reversals. Thanks to O'Shea's explanations, he could see the plan behind the murdered women, and the burning of Collins' meticulously documented accounts. He saw how the plan had been executed, how the events he had lived through over the past fortnight were all related, nothing stray or unconnected, like the snow itself, falling with concentrated steadiness, emanating from a single point of distant coldness. The human heart could be colder than any winter, he realised. One man in particular had spawned an overwhelming current of coldness, which he was following now, back to the source.

The flakes had stopped falling by the time he reached the foothills of the Wicklow Mountains. Isham's mansion glittered in the moonlight, beckoning him closer, like a palace built of ice. A groom was saddling up the corporal's grey horse; the clink of a bridle broke the muffled silence. Kant knew that Isham was roaming somewhere in the depths of the house. Everything stopped here, he realised. He had found the core of the labyrinth.

A footman opened the door for Kant and led him into a hall. Presently, Isham's tall figure appeared, faultlessly dressed in full riding gear, a whip in his hands, and an Irish red setter accompanying him. His face had a frozen quality, betraying neither surprise nor warmth at Kant's arrival.

'What do you want?' he asked.

'I'm looking for Lily Merrin.'

'Still?' Isham sounded exasperated.

'I suspect she might have come here.'

'That woman is a traitor. She operated outside the normal rules of society. She betrayed her country and orchestrated the abduction of a child.'

'Her child.'

'No matter. She deserves the death penalty.'

'I'm not leaving until I know she's safe.'

'Did you bring anyone with you?'

'No.'

'Who's helping you?' A thread of tension crept into his voice. The question was an important one.

'I work alone.'

Isham walked to the front door and stared out at the grounds of the estate. Apparently satisfied with Kant's response, he made an effort at courtesy. 'I marvel at where you get your persistence from.' The muscles of his face relaxed slightly. 'You'd better come and join me. I would like you to be my guest tonight on a midnight hunt. Just do your best not to get in the way when the hounds strike off.'

He led Kant into the hall and up a flight of stairs. The reporter feigned strength and good health, but he could not suppress his racking cough, and his shoulders stooped. Isham waited for him at the top of the stairs.

'I'm beginning to think you're not a man at all, Kant,' said Isham. 'More an illness. A spasm from the dank earth.'

They entered a sitting room on the first floor, where a fire was blazing merrily in the cavernous hearth. From the heat in the room, Kant deduced that the fire had been burning for some time. An untidy stack of papers and manuscripts sat beside the fire, like the pages of a massively sprawling book, some of which had been ripped out and thrown onto the fire. Isham lifted a wad of the papers, perused them briefly and flung them onto the fire.

'What sort of hunt takes place in the middle of the night?' asked Kant. He was nervous as to what Isham was planning, but his desire to ensure Merrin's safety was stronger than his fear.

'A hunt for wild creatures, vermin. I'm sick of sweeping the streets of rebels.'

'What kind of vermin?'

'A creature called the Irish woodkerne. Ever heard of it?' Isham's face gleamed in the firelight. 'The first Englishmen came across them in the 1600s.'

'What trouble have they been causing?'

'They have been a greater pest than usual this winter, which is why I have been going hard with the hounds. They come out of the darkness, without warning, leaping, venomous. I'll get the groom to saddle you up a horse.'

'I'm not here to chase animals. I'm hunting a murderer.'

Isham did not appear to have heard him. He marched off and barked some orders in the hallway below. He returned and rubbed his hands over the fire, the buckles of his riding jacket and boots shining. He lifted another bunch of the papers and let them drop one by one onto the fire, watching them burn and flap upwards in tatters of ash. The energy of the fire seemed to draught through him, feeding his eyes with a dangerous glow.

'Do you plan to burn all those papers?' asked Kant.

Isham lifted his face from the fire and looked round. 'Why, are you interested in reading them?' A sly look darkened his face. 'Come with me on my hunt, and afterwards I'll let you read what's left.'

'I've a better idea. You go on the hunt, and I'll stay and read.'

Isham laughed, the tension relaxing its hold on him, if only temporarily.

'You should read a little less, Mr Kant, and do some living.'

The hounds began to stir in the stables, and the tension returned to Isham.

He began walking back and forth to the window, flicking his whip against his thigh. He behaved like a wild creature himself, more aware of its own savage appetites than the presence of Kant. He lost interest completely in the stack of papers by the fire.

Kant joined Isham at the bay window. Below them, the moonlit yard, the grey horse, the motionless groom looked like an engraving in ice.

'We must rest awhile, Mr Kant. We have exertions ahead of us.'

Over the next hour, Isham's agitation increased. The fire burned brightly, throwing his restless shadow onto the high ceiling. He passed back and forth in front of the fireplace, flicking his whip in a series of masterful but sullen movements. Every now and again, he went over to one of the windows and peered into the darkness. Kant remained in the shadows beyond the firelight, anxious to keep the corporal under his surveillance.

Shortly after midnight, the setter scrambled to the door and began barking. The hounds in the stables answered with their sharp yelps. A look of relief fell across Isham's face.

'Follow me,' he said gruffly. 'The groom will have your mare ready. Riding a horse in the middle of the night is the most free you will ever feel.'

They descended a set of back stairs and walked out into the yard. Isham grabbed the reins and mounted his grey stallion. He spun his horse in tight circles as Kant climbed onto his mare.

'I promise you a spectacle, Mr Kant. A hunt you have dreamed of only in your darkest nightmares. Woodkerne are such rare and exciting quarry, a single specimen, ripe with fear, affords more pleasure than a dozen foxes.'

The groom opened the doors of the kennels, and the hounds poured out in a hungry frenzy, squirming and leaping around the horses.

'Look at them, the beauties,' cried Isham. 'They have been kept on such meagre rations they are starving. Grip with your knees and don't roll off, else my hounds will chop you with their fangs. I swear they'll tear you from your bones, to the very last mouthful.'

The pack of hounds struck off, reeling across the frozen grass like a squall. They veered one way and then another, before rippling into a dark plantation of fir trees. Isham was gone already, his horse hooked into their wake. Kant nudged his mount with his heels, and the mare surged after them. The snow grew deeper, the horse lunging through a spray of ice crystals. He could hear Isham's stallion pounding the ground, but could only catch a glimpse of his ghostly figure disintegrating in a cloud of churned up snow. Isham was right. For a moment, Kant felt a joyous sense of freedom and wanted to laugh. The air filled his lungs like pure oxygen. He had to remind himself of Isham's warning, that this was a prelude to a nightmare, not a fairy-tale ride through an enchanted forest.

Isham was waiting for him at the brow of a low hill. He looked exhilarated and his hair was disarrayed. His horse swayed slightly, ready to strike off again, at the merest signal from Isham.

'I wanted to ask you something, Kant. You're not obliged to answer me, of course.' He hesitated while he restrained his horse. 'Do you believe you are capable of love?'

'What do you mean?'

'Do you believe you are made to find happiness in the normal human terms – through a sexual relationship with a woman?' His voice was courteous but cold.

Kant's horse shied at something in the trees, its stumbling hooves pounding perfect crescents in the snow. Kant gripped the reins and hauled the horse's twisting neck into line. Isham's horse stood stock still, its head held to the wind.

'Do you know what that was?' asked Isham.

'I didn't hear a thing.'

'That was the woodkerne. The horses sense its fear.'

Both their mounts remained standing for a moment, then Isham led his stallion on.

'What matters to me is satisfaction,' continued Isham.

'And I can only find it in the opposite of love.' His voice grew hoarse. He seemed on the verge of confessing a shameful secret. 'We're alike, you and I, Kant. Neither of us can understand what it means to submit to peace. England is a foreign land to men like us. How do our comrades go back there and lead a normal life?'

'You'll never lead a normal life because you have submitted yourself to cruelty, your lust for power over women.'

'It's true. I am cruel and violent, at least in human terms. But, you should know that coming to terms with one's cruelty is one of the most magnificent experiments a man can conduct in his life. Most men never get to plumb the depths of their animal instincts, never satisfy their lust for violence. I've won that right. Awakening my instincts has become my overriding ambition. I want nothing more than the tumult and fury of the chase.'

The moon dipped behind the trees, and the night seemed to contract, enclosing Kant in a dense cell of shadows. His horse shook its head, and he steadied it with his reins. Ahead of them, he could hear the hunger of the hounds, an out-of-control pack, zigzagging through the trees.

The horses drew to a halt, again. Isham strained to listen, and the horses lengthened their necks, flicking their ears. Isham sidled his horse along a thicket of thorn trees and pointed to a set of crystal prints in the freshly fallen snow.

'Is it the woodkerne?' asked Kant.

'Correct. This one has cunning and resilience, which makes for good sport.'

Kant examined the prints. They looked like the blurred hoof marks of a pony.

'You haven't told me what sort of creature it is.'

'Woodkerne were people once. Before they became outlaws, fugitives from justice.'

The wintry twigs trembled under the weight of snow.

People? Was that what Isham had said? The stream of freezing air pummelled his thoughts. It took all his concentration to keep his reluctant horse moving. With his free hand, Isham bent a branch out of the way, and they pressed deeper into the forest.

'Do you know why I enjoy hunting by the moon?' Isham slowed his pace to accommodate Kant.

'It forces the human quarry to grope about in the undergrowth like animals. It makes them see like animals, run like animals, cry like animals. Beneath the snow, their bones litter the forest floor.'

The true horror of Isham's hunting parties had dawned on Kant. His tension was communicated unconsciously to his horse, which took off skittishly and had to be reined in tightly. Isham kept talking as naturally as if they were two riding companions distracting each other with entertaining stories. His finger-ends twitched all the time on the reins.

'The hounds and wild animals dispose of the bodies with great efficiency.'

Kant did not feel inclined to press him for further clarification but Isham was eager to talk.

'The first chase I was much too cautious. I made her run on foot with only a few minutes' head start, and the hounds caught her too quickly. I was left with too much mess to clear up before dawn and not enough time to enjoy the justice of her death.'

'Justice?'

'Yes. The sense of retribution. The hounds ensured their deaths were just as gruesome as I envisaged them.'

The memory of a secret delight glittered in his eyes. 'I was much more pleased with the hunts that followed. I decided to give the kerne a sporting chance. I even supplied them with ponies to test their riding skills.'

'How did you lure them into the forest?'

'I released them from prison and told them Collins wanted to meet them here at Park House. I made them take a vow of secrecy.'

Kant looked away. The branches of the fir trees swayed in the wind. He thought of Lily Merrin, making her way through the shadows, alone, waiting for a signal from Collins.

The moon rode clear of the trees and clouds, draining the parkland of its shadows, like a pale magnet of death. The hounds eddied across an open field, then climbed a hill towards a thicket of thorn trees. The horses followed at a canter. Kant focused on guiding his mount through the snow, but every now and again, he swivelled his head in horrified fascination to take in the rider alongside him, his face floating like a cold mask, a bird of prey with features perfectly still. How many women had he murdered?

Kant's horse grew more fretful and spooked. It shied at invisible objects, the subtlest shadows, while Isham's moved at ease, as if it knew the lie of the land with its eyes closed. Kant buried his heels into the flanks of his mount. He grew absorbed by the concentrated effort of riding, the freezing air sharp in his lungs. Gradually their horses took them to higher ground.

Now that he had revealed his secret, Isham showed a greater sense of ease. He turned his horse in an circle, the expression of his face serious and proud. Moonlight and shadow flickered across his features. With an exaggerated sense of ceremony, he removed a bugle from his belt and blew a series of long, piercing notes, and then he leaned out of his saddle and listened to the commotion of the hounds pouring back from the edge of the night.

'I am grateful you accepted my invitation tonight, Kant,' he said, his mouth quivering with pleasure. 'For weeks, I have felt like an artist who has carefully perfected a masterpiece and is overwhelmed by the need to show it to someone.'

The scrabbling pack broke through the trees and surrounded them. Isham urged them in the direction of a fresh set of hooves, which led into the thicket of thorns.

'Don't feel too sorry for Collins' female spies. They have an impulse towards death. How else could they resist my little midnight hunts?' He swung his horse so close to Kant, the reporter could smell the stallion's sweat. 'Collins didn't just choose these women because they were wonderfully adept secretaries. He picked them for their desperation and neediness. Just like the lust-murderers of Whitechapel who pick on the desperation of whores. Collins relied on a different form of desperation, that of young women made free by education and employment. He craved their secrets. The possession of their hearts. But when they were no longer useful to him, or imprisoned, he was content to let them rot in darkness.'

'What about Merrin?'

'She was the perfect prize. The widow of a British soldier. A member of the Protestant Ascendancy. Collins must have found the darkness of her secret as alluring as her beauty and breeding. It gave him a degree of intimacy with the enemy that would have been impossible in the normal rules of war. Merrin threatened to be his undoing.'

Kant pulled back his horse.

'You have grown reckless in satisfying your lust for cruelty. It is out of control and will destroy you.'

'True. The more I satisfy my lust for punishment, the worse it gnaws at me. I cannot satisfy it, no matter what I destroy in the act. However, you make the mistake that violence, the will to cruelty, is an instinct to be controlled. I've come to believe that it exists as an enormous, overarching life-force.'

The yelping of the hounds jolted them back to the moonlit tableau of thorns and banks of snow. They followed the dogs past trees lit up by the moon, in haloes of horror.

The hounds were intent on one particular thicket of thorns. They began to howl. The night changed its mood; the dome of the moon rising above the trees, lifted it seemed by the baying of the hounds. The pack grew more excited, circling and wheeling around the edge of the thicket. Isham rode into the pack, horse and man weaving back and forth amid their bristling bodies. He steadied his horse and made it stand absolutely still for several moments. The hounds began to whine and then grew quiet, too, their noses quivering, their breath smoking the air, their tongues lolling over their teeth. Kant coughed in the jagged air. From somewhere deep in the thicket, a branch cracked.

A rider on a pony bounded out of the thorns in front of them, took a plunging leap and cleared a row of bushes into a forest of pines. Even the hounds were stunned for a moment. Isham laughed, kicked his horse, and took off after the pony, following its path through the trees, leaning his horse one way and then another, gaining all the time on the galloping pony.

Kant caught a glimpse of Merrin's face as she rode the

pony deep into the forest. He saw her painful, haunted eyes as she glanced behind to check the closeness of her pursuers.

They rode hard towards the edge of the forest. In the distance, Kant could see a view of Dublin city, a fantasy of gaslights and freezing mists, huddling tenements and military bases, churches and alleyways and empty streets woven into a maze of shadows.

The perspective must have distracted Merrin's pony for it missed a hollow in the forest floor and buckled into the snow, sending Merrin flying out of her saddle. She was up and running instantly, but in the wrong direction. She slipped through the trees before Isham could turn his galloping horse, and ran towards Kant and the approaching hounds.

He reached a hand towards her bolting shape.

'It's me, Kant,' he shouted.

Fear made her eyes roll. She flung out her arm and he grabbed it. The lift was a continuation of her momentum, and he required less effort than he expected to swing her onto the saddle behind him. The movement of his horse knocked her face against his shoulder and neck. Her skin felt as cold as marble. He rode back the way they came through the pack of hounds, without thinking, his heels digging hard into the horse's sweating flanks. Sometimes it was better to let the body take over. All the time, he could sense the pounding of the grey stallion's hooves and the baying of the hounds drawing closer.

He heard the mechanics of a weapon being drawn, felt the nuzzle of a gun pressed against his ribs. He glanced behind at Merrin. Her eyes had lost their fear. His knees jarred against the horse as he tried to extend the gallop.

'It's me,' he shouted again.

'I know who you are.'

The gun pressed harder into his side. 'It's time you made an end to this pursuit of me.'

'Isham plans to kill you. He lured you here so his hounds could tear you apart.' He felt the hand holding the gun tremble.

'You keep following me like a shadow. I don't know where it's going to end.' She sighed with resignation, as though coerced into being saved.

She dug the weapon harder into his side, steadied herself, then swung the gun round at Isham's gaining figure. Her hand shook with the motion of the horse, but somehow she managed to carefully ease the hammer and shoot.

In spite of her careful aim, the bullet struck the overhanging branch of a tree. The shot reverberated through the forest, followed by a moment's silence and then came the crack of bark splitting, the snow-laden branch straining, and tumbling through the air. Kant glanced behind and saw it swipe the nose of Isham's horse before hitting the ground. The stallion, startled, crashed sideways through several more branches, knocking Isham to the side of the animal's neck. He clung on for several galloping strides and then slid further. In spite of his horsemanship, Isham lost his seat completely and fell to the ground, one foot still hooked in a stirrup. He still held the reins but his efforts just made the horse wheel around him. A wild rage took hold of him as he struggled to control the animal, but it was dragging him now. He fell to hopping alongside the flanks of the stallion, like a child in the throes of a desperate game of hop-scotch. His standing leg grew weak, faltered. He pulled harder on the reins but the horse, hearing the approaching yelping of the hounds, spun round in tighter circles of panic.

The pack caught up with them quickly, lobbing themselves

over the stricken horse, seeking their quarry. Their loose bellies made them look almost weightless in the moonlight. Most of the pack seemed to recognise that Isham was their master, and pressed on, but one or two of the younger dogs attacked him in the frenzy. Isham seemed to cough each time the hounds struck him. The rest of the pack turned at the smell of blood, their hunger overcoming any bonds of loyalty. Isham's face looked astonished, furious, as the impact of their piling bodies knocked him to the ground. The lead hound pulled him by the throat. He grappled with it, his face fixed in a snarl. The spittle in his mouth turned red, began to froth and bubble, and his arms released their hold of the hound, swaying in the air like a drowning man waving for help.

Kant felt a tremor of terror run through Merrin's body. He backed his horse away. All the fight had gone from Isham. He dwindled under the hounds, a sack of flesh pulled to pieces, his blood lust finally consummated in his own death.

The moon rode alongside them as they galloped back to the mansion, swelling and then shrinking, vanishing behind clouds and trees, and then reborn in a clear sky, lighting up a crystal path for them through the snow. He heard a sigh from Merrin.

'Are you cold?' he asked.

'No,' she replied. 'It's the moon and the snow...' She allowed the rest of her explanation to slip away.

They rode on in silence. He wanted nothing now but this shared sense of escape, the two of them leaning into the onrushing face of the night, nothing but this lucid and excited flight from death. He knew he was not made for love or ordinary family life, but that neither would he submit to the dark and terrible forces Isham had served.

His mind returned to that bewildering moment in the darkened carriage when her body went limp against his. Not daring to breathe, wondering what would happen next. It must have been the pressure of her body behind him, the darkness and the smell of the horse that made him think of that afternoon again. It all came flooding back. The thin crack of daylight, the shaking of the horses' harness, her blurred face drawing closer, the lips offering his mouth a kiss that seemed like a secret message he could not interpret.

His astonishment and curiosity as to whom she had mistaken him for had set him loose on a journey of sudden turns and unexpected conspiracies. All the events of the past fortnight crystallised around that single kiss. He recalled the sense of strangeness as she pressed upon his mouth, her lips freezing and then the sudden recoil at his reserve, the curtain pulled back and the look of shock in her face. He knew he was not made for such a kiss. It had not been his to receive. It had left him wandering the streets of Dublin, hungry in every sense, the memory of their encounter the only light flickering in the darkness.

They kept riding through the night. He looked up at the black sky, and a pattern of snowflakes came soaring out of the darkness, planting themselves on his tingling face, like blind arrows, like misdirected kisses.

They dismounted in the stable yard and hurried into the warmth of the mansion. Upstairs the fire had dwindled to smouldering embers. Beside it, the pile of papers lay intact.

'That afternoon in the hansom cab, you thought I was Mick Collins,' he said.

She made a vague gesture with her hands. 'I was beginning

to think the world had forgotten me, until you turned up with your silver cane. I had confided everything in Collins, you see. For the first time, that afternoon I wanted to truly lean on him. I wanted to kiss him because I was sick with fear and loneliness. It was a coincidence that I found you instead.'

Kant wanted to say that there were no coincidences in life.

'You ensured that the file wouldn't fall into the wrong hands,' he said. 'Perhaps we were meant to meet. Some force unbeknownst to us brought us together.'

'The same forces that almost killed us', she replied. 'Money and greed.'

She knelt at the bundle of papers, Mick's great work of describing and cataloguing a revolution.

'I thought you'd be sick of those files by now,' remarked Kant. 'Isham was trying to send them all to heaven where nothing more would ever be seen of them.'

'I want to read them one more time, and touch their secrets.'

Kant joined her by the fire and began flicking through the documents. The wind gusted and blew a cloud of smoke down the chimney. He retreated, coughing harshly, and a horde of soot flakes swirled into the room, falling around the figure of Lily, who was busy untying the remaining bundles.

He watched as she went through the papers. From time to time, she rubbed her brow to help focus her concentration. He was afraid to say anything or move in case it would distract her. She opened a bundle of documents, seemingly at random, and scanned through the pages. She took another, and then another, scrutinising the pages hurriedly until she had examined most of the stack. By her side, she had gathered a small pile of pages.

She looked up at him in surprise and pointed to a series of scribbles that had been added to the documents.

'They look like the pencil markings of an idle hand,' said Kant.

She shook her head.

'They're part of Mick's secret code. He has examined these accounts and picked out some sort of pattern associated with O'Shea's signature. He has tracked the transactions back over the past six months.'

He saw that, amid the indecipherable marks, Collins had placed a black dot next to O'Shea's signature on several sets of the accounts. What did the dots represent? Since Collins the master bureaucrat had made them, they must have had something to do with time or control or money. The former civil servant's delight in documenting something secret, a little stream of information kept hidden from everyone else.

'They must mark the time and place when something exceptional happened,' she said. 'Something calculated and secret.'

Kant sat hunched over the files, examining them in detail, feeling that he was close to the dark heart of a conspiracy. O'Shea had instructed Isham to burn the files. There had been an urgency about his actions, even tonight, before the hunt, which suggested a degree of panic. Why hadn't he and O'Shea just dropped out of circulation and gone on the run? Why were the files still so important, long after the money had been siphoned off?

'You can't hide secrets from Mick,' said Merrin. 'He finds out everything, even the darkest plots against him.'

Kant stared at the pages. The most recent transaction

marked by Collins was a payment for the chartering of a boat from Bray harbour. He looked at the date. It was due to leave at dawn the next morning.

'What if Isham had been told to burn the files so as to cover up a grand crime that took place not sometime in the past but in the future?'

'We're not fortune tellers,' she replied. 'How can we predict what's going to happen in the future?'

He waved the page he was holding. 'O'Shea has signed for a boat to leave Bray harbour tomorrow morning. The *Cygnet* has been chartered to sail in one direction only, across the Irish Sea to Wales. Why would the IRA need a boat to sail to the mainland but not return?'

'They use boats to smuggle weapons to Ireland. Surely, they're not smuggling the weapons back?'

'What if something else is being transported to the mainland? Something more destructive than guns and bullets. What if the boat is delivering a bomb?'

He let the page fall among the ashes. 'Wars are unpredictable. Like people. One never knows how they're going to turn out.'

TWENTY-FIVE

The sea air was softening the grimy darkness when Kant arrived with Merrin at the harbour. He felt light-headed from the lack of sleep and the novelty of having her at his side. Merrin agreed to keep watch at the harbour entrance in case of an ambush, while Kant pressed on, hoping that his weary feet would lead him to his dawn rendezvous with the *Cygnet* and its crew.

He followed the cries of the seagulls to the far corner of the harbour. He felt as though he was weaving his own walkway through the darkness, like a spider scuttling across a vast web. The spear-like masts of moored boats pierced the gloom, their tonnage nestling close to him as he hurried across the walkway. The sea swelled over the harbour walls, foam seething in the dawn light. Somewhere in the dim light, the blast of a ship horn signalled a departure or arrival.

It was almost dawn, that in between time of the day, when shadows turn to solid objects. His mind raced to complete the shapes before they fully emerged from the retreating gloom. Out of the overlapping silhouettes, he connected a sail here, to a stern there. In the same way, he tried to connect the events of the past week. His thinking was more like dreaming, and there was a lot of material to churn through. Why was there just one man on board? What was he loading onto the yacht? Guns? A bomb destined for London? The yacht took shape, shimmering with gold at its edges, swaying slightly in the water. Shadows drained from the boat; a porthole window burned with the light of the rising sun.

His suspicions had a single, clear subject now. The dawn light intensified, and out of the murk rose the figure of O'Shea, standing alone on the deck of his yacht. He was dressed in a thick sea-faring jumper and moleskin coat, grinning at the sooty dawn with a daring that had put him beyond the reach of Dublin Castle and Collins' squad. All that desperate searching for a set of accounts, all those incoherent conspiracies swirling in the air, boiled down to this one act of audacious theft.

'Mr Kant, you've come early to see me off.' O'Shea seemed full of good humour.

He swung a final wooden crate into the boat's hold. It clattered heavily below.

'Throwing around explosives like that is not a good idea,' said Kant.

O'Shea laughed. Whatever he was transporting, it wasn't bombs.

Kant wondered where the rest of the crew was. It didn't seem feasible that O'Shea was carrying out a smuggling operation single-handedly. O'Shea seemed reluctant to leave. His grin bordered on a taunt.

'Be sure and say goodbye to Mick for me.'

Daylight revealed an urgency in the sky, dark clouds crowding in from the east. Against the backdrop of an approaching storm, O'Shea stood as still as a statue.

'Is this it?' Kant raised his voice. 'You're leaving Ireland. What about the revolution? I thought there was money to be made. What about all those opportunities you talked about?'

The light of sunrise was submerged in the gathering gloom.

'Believe me, I've been waiting months for this particular opportunity.'

He removed a gun from his jacket pocket and levelled it at Kant. 'I'm taking away Mick's little treasure trove. The remainder of the National Loan that he converted into gold coins. With so much money washing in, Collins was afraid Dublin Castle would seize the cash if it were left sitting in bank accounts. He arranged for it to be converted into gold and hidden away. Which was very inconvenient for a businessman like me.'

'Why inconvenient?'

'Don't you know your economics? Idle capital is a destructive force. It drives the economy down a very slippery slope to ruin. Every single ha'penny should be in circulation, not locked away in secret chests. It became much harder to get my hands on the cash.' O'Shea took aim at Kant with his revolver. 'No one is going to stop me now. Certainly not a snooping reporter.'

'But you've made mistakes. Big mistakes. You've left a trail of evidence that will point Collins in your direction.'

'You're stalling for time, Mr Kant.'

'Not getting rid of me earlier was a mistake. Instead you tipped me off about Isham.'

'I needed you to answer some questions. Like how much you and Merrin knew about my little smuggling plans, and whether you'd told anyone else. Whether Collins would be waiting for me at this harbour. Until I found out those answers I still had some need of you. Tipping you off about Isham was a way of sidelining you. I knew you'd go running to rescue Merrin.'

'If you don't believe that was an error, then I'll tell you a more serious mistake. Isham didn't burn all the account files. I've examined them. Mick knows you've chartered this boat for a one-way journey to England. He marked the transaction with a black dot.'

O'Shea paused for thought. For the first time, he looked capable of being surprised, of being wrong-footed. He looked at the entrance to the harbour, scanning the shadows for signs of life. All was quiet apart from the mewling of the gulls. His face assumed a calculatedly blank expression.

'Perhaps Ireland's military mastermind was doodling before he fell asleep.'

'No. He's been keeping your transactions under surveillance.' Kant spoke quickly, wanting to build on O'Shea's growing uncertainty. He began edging sideways to a tin storehouse. 'He's tracked them back. It might not be days from now, or weeks, but Collins will come after you. He'll simply appear at your bedside in the middle of the night with a gun raised to your head.'

O'Shea shrugged his shoulders and fired the revolver at Kant, who ducked for cover. The bullet struck him in his left arm, the impact knocking him to the ground. O'Shea jumped from the boat and stood over him with the gun. Kant closed his eyes, waiting for the shot. When it came, he was surprised to feel no pain. Another shot rang out, and this time he recognised the retort of a rifle from further along the harbour. He looked up in time to see the grin on O'Shea's face shrink back into his skull. The insurance manager's hands groped at two buds of deep red that were blossoming through tears in his moleskin coat. Like rotten sacking, he slumped to the ground, blood gurgling from the wounds.

The profiles of three men emerged from a tarpaulin covering a nearby boat. The metal sheen of their guns gave them away. They slinked from the inky darkness of the boat onto the pier. The only sound Kant heard was the gulping of saltwater against the moored boats. He watched their gleaming eyes approach, their looming figures silhouetted against the murky dawn. Kant recognised the shoes worn by the lead shadow. Smartly polished and made of the finest French leather. It was Mick Collins and two of his henchmen. Collins ignored Kant and stood over O'Shea's body. He spoke in a language Kant did not understand. It might have been a prayer or a curse. The strange syllables made it hard to determine whether anger or regret was the dominant tone.

'Did you hear what O'Shea told me?' asked Kant when Collins had finished talking over the dead body.

Collins looked straight at him and the light in his eyes became more intense.

'His confession? Every word of it.' He smiled stiffly at Kant.

'Did you know he was planning to clean out the IRA's finances?'

'Why does it matter now?'

'It matters to me'

Collins looked at him with interest. 'How?'

'So that I can report what happened here.'

Collins smiled and nodded. 'I was hoping you'd come along and see his greedy little escape bid for yourself. A crime like this needs an objective observer, someone to put the record straight.'

His henchmen lifted O'Shea's body and heaved it into the water. His arms were the last part of him to disappear, giving what looked like a tired little wave before sinking beneath the waves.

'When did you discover his conspiracy?'

Collins shrugged. 'Even a conceited gombeen from Cork can't be fooled forever. O'Shea's mistake was to involve himself with a madman like Isham. His mistake but my good fortune. His murderous scheme will embarrass Dublin Castle as much as it will the republican movement.'

'Why didn't you stop him earlier? You had ample opportunity.'

'I didn't want to move against him until the trap was fully set. He wasn't the only enemy from within I had to contend with.'

'Brugha?'

'That's right, Mr Kant. In the end, Brugha did me the greatest favour, carrying round that briefcase as though it was the trigger of my destruction. It forced me to go back over all the accounts.' Collins watched as his men clambered onto the boat and began unloading the crates of gold. 'The books are clean now, and Brugha has lost his grubby little hold of history. He and the hardliners in the army council will be sidelined now, and the IRA will follow my vision.'

Kant could see Collins' brilliance as a strategist, using Brugha's accusations to weed out the malcontents in the IRA's ruling council, the colleagues who held secret grievances against him, or misgivings about his military leadership. They had united behind Brugha and his crazy plot to discredit Collins, and now their positions had been exposed and undermined.

'Revolutions are dangerous things. There's the enemy without and the enemy hiding within. Every now and again, one has to smoke the bastards out. Brugha will have to live with the realisation that all his efforts have only strengthened my position.'

He removed a gun from his jacket pocket. 'I feel like I've been trying to bid you goodbye forever, Mr Kant.'

'I was hoping you might give up.'

'On the contrary, I'm going to try one more time.' He let the weapon dangle in his hand. 'You've earned another two days on your account, no more.'

'What account?'

'I want you gone by St Stephen's Day. There's a mail boat leaving Dublin harbour at midnight. Be sure to be on it.'

Like a bare dagger, the rising sun forced its way through the storm clouds, filling the harbour pier with glinting light. To Kant, the patch he was standing on felt like the brightest place on earth. Watching Collins walking away, he thought how much he would miss the darkness of the Dublin nights, the refuge of shadows and gloom. The morning leaned closer, magnified by the reflective sea, the salt air stinging his eyes.

As Collins suggested, he had his ticket booked for the boat by that same evening, but he was not yet ready to make his exit. He met Lily Merrin one final time on the empty promenade along the beach at Bray. It was twilight and the gas lamps had not yet been lit when she arrived. He almost did not recognise her in the fading light, dressed in an elegant white dress and wrapped in a fur coat. She seemed more alone than she had ever been before, standing in front of him without removing her hands from her pockets.

'At last, we're in the clear,' she said.

'Part of me wishes we were back in the dark,' he replied.

They went for a long walk, dodging the waves that

came frowning over the promenade. He walked with more urgency than she did, turning towards her, gesticulating as he spoke. He was trying to persuade her to leave Dublin and join him on the mail boat to Liverpool, but the roar of the waves kept drowning his voice, and she kept turning her face in the opposite direction.

'I must tell you my fears for you and your son,' he shouted. 'You are at the edge of a precipice. All that remains for you in this country is darkness and danger. Come away with me to London. There you will be free of history and politics.'

She turned to him, unable to look him in the eye, her face wearing the faintest expression of sorrow. 'If we leave Ireland, we will leave defeated. And my son will taste that defeat for the rest of his life. This road we are taking may be the wrong one, but it is ours to take. I know you mean well, but you are not the rescuer I need. Not now.'

'I'm pleading with you to think of your son and his future.'

She gave his hand a final squeeze, and walked away without looking back.

The thought of losing her now, after she had dominated his thoughts for so long, frightened him almost to death. He called out her name one last time but his voice choked. He stared at her retreating figure, unable to tear himself away.

The dim stretch of beach fell away to churning darkness. He felt the cold touch of the sea on his cheeks. He listened to the labour of the waves, grinding against the pebbles piled to protect the beach, each wash lasting as long as his breath. His doomed breath. The darkness was everywhere, stretching away unbearably. He knew he would have to adjust to this separation so he gave up looking back at her.

He walked away from the promenade to a small church that had opened its doors for the Christmas vigil mass.

The charge of the waves against the beach was replaced by something else, the chanting of the faithful as they recited the rosary.

The mass goers crowded around him as he entered the church doors, pressing against him with a steadfast force. They were families who had emerged from freezing terraces, their faces in shadow, ragged clothing wrapped around them in layers, their half-sleeping children staggering around their legs. He listened to their praying voices filling the candle-lit interior, praying for the blind, praying for the prisoners, praying for everyone who was lost and lonely. He felt the flow of emotion and faith from their lips, mouthing the same prayers repeatedly, offerings to a God hiding in the darkness. It occurred to him that, if he concentrated hard, he could hide himself amid them, fill the gaping shadows of their faces with the ghost of himself, be one with them, inhabit their bodies, and grow to understand how they could create faith and devotion out of this infinite darkness. He joined in the prayers, following their repetitive words, his voice gaining strength, his chest swelling, his loneliness rising up like a final roar of love.

THE END

AUTHOR'S NOTE

Although Michael Collins survived the allegations of financial impropriety, Cathal Brugha continued his pursuit of the IRA leader until his death, dragging in Eamon de Valera, the rest of the Irish Republican leadership, and eventually the Irish parliament. The scandal took its toll on Collins, whose appearance began to betray his ill-health. A British Intelligence report from the time gave the following description of him: "Must have been a powerful man a few years ago, now heavy in movement and greatly out of condition."

Despite his ill-health, Collins tried to bring about a truce in December 1920 that would have saved many lives, but he was unwilling to take the political risks necessary. He went on to lead the Irish delegation at the peace conference in London which resulted in the Anglo-Irish Treaty of December 1921. This brought the Irish Free State into existence and partitioned the island, with six predominantly Unionist counties in the north remaining outside the Free State. The Treaty was passed by the cabinet in Dublin by one vote. On 22 August 1922, Collins was assassinated by anti-treaty forces in an ambush in County Cork.

Letters between Collins and Moya Llewelyn Davies were

captured by Dublin Castle in 1921 and she was briefly jailed before being deported to Britain. Collins was worried while she was in prison and sent flowers to her daily. Once the truce was declared, she returned to Dublin and took a room in the Gresham Hotel where Collins had his headquarters. Claiming to have spied on behalf of Collins, she annoyed people around Collins by her claims to be at the 'heart' of the revolution. Later in life, she added that she and Collins had been lovers. She died a lonely and vulnerable woman, her remains buried in an unmarked grave in Deansgrange Cemetery, Dublin.

About Us

In addition to No Exit Press, Oldcastle Books has a number of other imprints, including Kamera Books, Creative Essentials, Pulp! The Classics, Pocket Essentials and High Stakes Publishing > oldcastlebooks.co.uk

For more information about Crime Books go to > crimetime.co.uk

Check out the kamera film salon for independent, arthouse and world cinema > kamera.co.uk

For more information, media enquiries and review copies please contact Frances > frances@oldcastlebooks.com